LOSING LOVE

A NOVEL

B.J. HERRON

Design and distribution by Bublish, Inc.

ISBN: 978-1-64704-484-8 (paperback)
ISBN: 978-1-64704-485-5 (hardback)
ISBN: 978-1-64704-483-1 (eBook)

For Granny & Nanny

Thank you for showing me what unconditional love looks like and why embracing my womanhood is a necessity.

Darkness.

Faith slept soundlessly. There was no tossing or turning tonight. For once, she didn't lie in bed worrying about her mother, who was snoring nearby. For the first time, Faith was certain that her mother would live to see the next day. She smiled, believing this was the beginning of something better.

She was wrong.

"Faith!"

She jumped out of bed. The sound of her mother's voice screaming her name filled the house.

"Faith, help me!"

Her small feet desperately tried to keep up with the rest of her small frame as Faith leapt out of bed. Her breath was hot and sweat dripped down her face as she descended the stairs.

She slowed at the sight of a man in black with his hands clasped around her mother's throat. Her mother desperately gasped for air as her eyes rolled into the back of her head.

Faith froze.

The stranger leaned up at the sight of the small child, keeping his pit bull-like grip on her mother's throat. The look on his face said he did not intend to let go.

He reached within his jacket, pulled out a gun, and aimed it at Faith. The child wished that she could find her voice, but somehow it had abandoned her. Just like she felt her mother had done, yet again. The strange man cocked the gun and then pulled the trigger.

BOOM!

CHAPTER 1

ABRUPT AWAKENING

know it isn't right. How I only allow him to dive so deep before stopping him from getting lost in what still has me trapped. For years now, I've succeeded in sharing just enough with him. I fear, however, that reign is coming to an end. I've watched my husband's impatience grow like a sickly person watches a lump on their body that they refuse to acknowledge. After seven years of marriage, it's not that I don't trust Nicholi. I do. I just don't want him to bear or feel my pain. And lose him as a result. Even now, I can feel him standing on the other side of the bathroom door. His big brown eyes alert. Brows furrowed with concern. His breathing even. Measured. Composed. He is immovable where he stands. I squeeze the edges of the marble vanity as tightly as I possibly can. The hot towel on my face hasn't calmed me down much. Frustrated, I cast it aside, giving myself a once-over in the oval-shaped mirror. The heavy bags underneath my eyes say *I am* more than tired.

Nicholi's tired, too. He hasn't been sleeping well, and my night terrors have interrupted his slumber for the third time this week. He needs to rest but won't. Not until I return to him, our bedroom, our bed, and am in his arms. I open the door, locking eyes with his. A glowing moon casts his 6-foot-3-inch frame across our bedroom. The floor creaks as he shifts his 220 pounds from his left to his right foot. He runs his big, sun-kissed hands through his scruffy hair. He's let it grow out a bit like the younger guys these days—and there are no complaints on my end. The rise and fall of his chest matches mine. We inhale, then exhale long and deep. Nicholi has stayed with me through everything. The trust issues. Mommy and daddy issues. Family issues. Honestly, just all the damn issues and years of therapy and night terrors. Long story short, I haven't made anything easy for him. For us. Fortunately, he is patient. Willing. And a damned good teacher. When Nicholi came along, I was praying for less chaos and confusion. To have a man genuinely care and love me? It felt as if I was learning a foreign language. All I understood was bullshit, miscommunication, and emotional manipulation.

That was Kent. He was my kryptonite. His lilt wrapped around my body like fine silk. He wouldn't let anyone hurt me because that was his job, right? But that's another story for another time. Nicholi was much different from Kent. He was healthy. He could watch me shine and not feel threatened. He reassured me when my anxiety skyrocketed. He affirmed me daily, was thoughtful, and an unselfish and loyal lover. He was present, listened, and knew when to let me take charge. His energy was unmatched. Most important, his actions mirrored his words. I trusted him, which was no small feat. That's why

I'd follow him anywhere: I trust that he will lead me in the right direction.

So, for the first time, I fell in love with the man and not the orgasm. It was refreshing. Mental stimulation. Doting compliments. An eagerness to keep him as satiated as he did me beyond the physical. Time stood still when we were together. We laughed from our bellies. Shared poetry. Freestyled when the spirit moved us. It was a true, consistent vibe. One that I had not experienced before, but also wasn't even aware that I needed. He'd finally asked me out after we kept running into each other in the library. I had spied him watching me for some time before then. Anyway, turns out he was in medical school to be a neurosurgeon and he learned I was studying law. Eventually we started studying together, and after a while, nothing felt right without him.

"Why are you here?" he asked after a couple of months of dating. We were at his off-campus apartment watching LeBron and the Cavaliers play Harden and the Rockets. I sat on the worn beige couch wearing his Princeton crewneck that swallowed me. He sat just a few feet away in his favorite black armchair in his usual sweatpants and T-shirt. Nicholi was irritated with me. I saw it in the way he winced. The way he pursed those full, pink lips of his. He rolled the blunt in his hands with precision. It seemed to ease his mind as he licked the papers. I couldn't fault him for being irritated. An old flame had called the day prior, triggering the fuck out of me. And here I was taking it out on the man that had me way too open to be open. Ironically, Whitney sang in the background about if she ran to someone would they stay or run away. I pondered what would Nicholi do.

"I know I haven't committed to you, but I'm here with a purpose," he said.

I started to ask exactly what that purpose was, but I couldn't find the words. It was a fresh line, but my heart bounded in that moment. He had proven significantly different from anyone else in my past.

"So what, you want to be friends?" He asked, defensive.

"No."

"Well, shit, what do you want?"

I wanted to tell him that after only two weeks of dating I saw both the beauty and chaos our passion could create. The latter would never truly surface because we would constantly bathe in the former. We already chose each other daily. There was no need for anyone else. How could I tell him that, after two weeks of dating, I knew our love could move mountains? Could literally heal anyone's heartache if they watched us pour into one another long enough. Could inspire one to love again by the amount of trust we had in each other. I knew that if we had children our ceiling would be their floor. There would be no obstacles, only doors that could be opened. After two weeks of dating, I saw all the ways I could transform for this man. From an unsure caterpillar to a gorgeous butterfly that knew no limits. He made me feel secure. Because of that I knew I could give this man whatever he needed. The lump in my throat, however, kept me from spilling my heart's desires. Instead, I found myself straddling him with the fullest intent of stepping outside of my comfort zone and the bullshit I'd come to know, understand, and expect from men. If I wanted better, I had to be better as well. No matter how arduous it was. No matter how scared I was. Shit, I deserved real satisfaction and bliss. All I could do was try.

"I want you and what we have," I said.

I held my husband's gaze as we stood in the frame of our bathroom door. Here we were, nearly a decade later. It wasn't perfect, but he was mine and had no reason to question if I was his.

"Breathe, Faith." His fingers caressed my face, cheeks, then outlined my lips which found his hands before they returned to the small of my back. The clock on our bedside table said it was a quarter past midnight.

"It's been a few months since your last episode. The other night could've been a trigger for you. You ready to talk about it?" He held my hands delicately. "Vault?"

This was our way of sharing the words we couldn't even whisper to others.

"Vault," I agreed, taking a beat. "Can my granny come live with us? She deserves peace, and to be selfish, at this stage of her life."

"I agree. And Philly would be good for her. If she wants to come, we'll make sure she's comfortable."

A second hadn't even passed before my lips found his. "We're in this together. Always." He caressed my face. "I also overheard you and Pat conversing about Terrell. Is that why you want to move her in?"

"Time. Please, babe."

Nicholi nodded his head in agreement.

I eyed my husband's solid frame. Sleep wasn't coming anytime soon, and although I knew a few ways to kill time, I'd already kept him up long enough.

"I'm gonna get some water."

"I'll come with you." He moved quick, searching for his loafers. "It's almost time for me to get up anyway."

"And that's all the more reason why you should get whatever rest you can. I'll be back in time."

3:21 a.m. Nicholi's alarm every morning since I've known him. The first time he stayed over, his siren startled me awake. When he didn't move, I lay back on my side, facing his broad back and shoulders. His sigh said he didn't want to move. Wanting to ease his mind, I rubbed his back until he found the strength to get up. He damn near begged me not to do the same once he was dressed. But I couldn't not see him out. It was certainly a sight to see. Watching him move so mechanically while his thoughts rang loud. He sat on my torn leather couch, laced up his sneakers, and sat as still as a rock for a few minutes. Finally, he noticed me in the shadows. His eyes beckoned me. So, I sat on his lap. It was so organic, the way I wrapped my right arm around him and he pulled me close at the waist with his left. Massaging the back of his head, planting soft kisses on his forehead and temple, preparing him to go out into a world that doesn't even truly appreciate him. I'd never responded to a man like this before. It became our morning ritual. All these years later and I still rise before the sun to let him know he's seen and loved before he walks out of the door.

After two glasses of water, I crept down the hallway and made a beeline for my study. It was my favorite part of the house because it was filled with books. Literally. I'd had an affinity for reading for as long as I could remember. Little did I know as a child that reading would provide an escape from my reality. I'd had three of my Earl Grey walls redesigned into 12 seven-story bookshelves. All were filled mostly with African American literature and memoirs. I scanned the shelves until I found *Harry Potter and the Order of the Phoenix*. First, don't judge me. It's one of the best written fiction books ever. It also featured my favorite bird, the phoenix. I always found the mythical bird empowering. Its ability to rejuvenate itself and rise anew from ashes was wildly inspiring and served as the motivation for everything I endured growing up with a substance-abusing mother; frequently incarcerated father; and crazy-ass family. Turning on the table lamp beside me, Granny's photo fell to the floor. We're at Tennessee State University for my graduation, and she is beaming with pride.

Yesterday should've been one of the happiest days of my life. I've been at Hughes & Smithe, one of the most prestigious law firms in the country, for nine years, junior partner for the past two. I was assigned a new high-profile case and my boss says that if I win there's a very good chance of being named partner. It was all because of Winifred Brooks on *A Different World*. She was my favorite character because she was an underdog. People didn't pay too much attention to her as she did them, but after coming into her own, nothing could stop her. They tried to clown her when she came back with that slick-ass bun and powerhouse suit. When she stood firm and said, "I am about something," baby, I was hooked. In that moment I decided to follow her footsteps. She was for her people, spoke with fervor, and stood for something. The high I was riding came to an abrupt halt after dinner when my sister, Patience, called to share that Granny had been arguing with her son, Terrell, again. My fifty-seven-year-old uncle, who lacks the will to work legally, had moved out of her home just two months ago.

"Granny needs a change of scenery, but you know she ain't going anywhere."

Pat's words lingered in the air. I agreed that Granny definitely deserved to live without any worries at her age.

"In the meantime, you should come home next weekend. We can take Granny to get massages and stuff. Hope would also love to see her aunt in person before the year's end. Your big-head brother, too. That's another conversation."

"Have you talked to your mother about him?"

"Cat ain't been around the past week for me to talk to. But Aunt Shirley say she popped up at her house a couple of days ago. She say she okay."

I was embarrassed not to have visited home since March, which was also the last time I spoke with my mother. It wasn't the best conversation. Here we were in August.

"Well, she always turns up, right? I want to see all of you, especially Eli to check on him. I have to be in L.A. in a couple of weeks for this new case. If I win, I'll make partner. You know how much I want that."

"I know," she chuckled. "You were studying for the LSAT in junior high. We just want to spend some time with you."

My fingers grazed the photograph once more. I cracked open *The Order of the Phoenix* for the thousandth time, trying to escape from thoughts of returning to Chicago.

CHAPTER 2
CRYSTAL CLEAR

Dr. Reese Tucker was a peculiar woman. Her crooked smile and seen-it-all eyes told me she had a fascinating story of her own. What's more, she resembled Jacqueline Broyer from *Boomerang* minus the over teased hair. And since we're there, she wasn't the villain at all—Jacqueline was, however, karma for Marcus's trash ass. Moving along, Dr. Tucker was beautiful. Even now, wearing a charcoal double-breasted skirt suit with matching heels, she looked effortless. You'd think that after four years of seeing her as my therapist I wouldn't be impressed anymore. Just like our sessions, she never disappoints.

"Making partner has been a big dream of yours." She tapped a pencil on the edge of her mahogany desk. "When do you leave?"

"In a few weeks. I'm thinking of going home for a weekend to visit before."

I eyed the photographs of her kids for the millionth time. A chocolate baby girl with big brown eyes and a head full of curly hair licking a lollipop three times her size. Her son was all dimples and eyelashes posing in his peewee soccer uniform in another photo. It was amazing that she was able to pop out not one, but two kids as she pursued her career. I envied her. Between Nicholi's career and mine, we hadn't had time to start our own family. Or perhaps we just hadn't made time? My lips pursed in speculation.

"How does that make you feel?"

I felt nauseated. You'd think it would be a breeze conversing about my issues with her after four years, but that wasn't the case. Expressing myself has never been my strong suit.

"I feel like I should be over this shit by now. I'm thirty-two. All of this happened more than fifteen years ago." My hands ran lazily across the leatherbound books on her desk. "I'm stronger, smarter. I'm not some innocent child desperately seeking her mother's love anymore."

"But you still want it, Faith. No matter what void your grandparents tried to fill, and nothing on the outside can heal those wounds, not all the books you read, or Nicholi, or making partner."

"Per usual, you're right. Being home just brings everything flooding back. It's emotionally draining, exhausting, and just not a healthy place for me."

"I understand that." Dr. Tucker scribbled on her note pad. "Maybe it's time you try to change that. And I think it starts with your relationship with your mother. You've shared your numerous failed attempts over the years to repair your relationship with her. You said she denied many things, but in the moments she's tried with you, were you receiving?"

"Come on now, Doc. You know I have."

"Have you? Remember, you told me for a long time you were dismissive, cold, and unresponsive." She leaned in for effect. "My point is that it takes two. Both of you have to be amicable and cooperative to make things work. I think you should try again."

Her Apple desktop chimed. She checked her chrome watch with a beautifully arched eyebrow. "My next appointment is here. Listen, I know you've never liked always being the bigger person. But remember that someone has to be."

Nicholi handed me a glass of Cabernet and insisted I go freshen up while he finished preparing dinner. I didn't object because that man had some serious skills in the kitchen. Plus, he was just a sweetheart like that. After all these years, I was still amazed that he found the time to plan date nights, weekend getaways, and vacations despite our workloads. He always made time for us, so I did the same. But we still hadn't started a family yet, and we both wanted children. Dr. Tucker's beautiful kids resurfaced in my mind. She and her husband had made it happen. Twice. Of course, it was none of my business. But I couldn't help but wonder if their children were planned or not. And no shade if they weren't. I leaned against the island, sipping my wine. Perhaps I should've prioritized children over realizing my dream of a custom-designed closet. Nicholi still teases me about it from time to time. Honestly, it was a bit pretentious, but it was very necessary. I gauged the grandiose room. Olive green walls with silver and white accents. Countless clothes, bags, trench coats, silk robes, and shoes arranged by color, season, and style. Full-length mirrors

ensure I was seen at all times under the ambi-
And the marble island was my centerpiece.
d Dr. Tucker's children were ours. Josie and I
hours in here playing dress-up and when we'd
finally chosen our outfits, we'd have a fashion show and
make her father and brother, Josiah, watch. Nicholi refused
to name him a junior because he wanted our son to have
his own identity. Josie would cheer for her brother at his
peewee soccer games while sitting on her papa's lap. My
husband would also have to tell me to calm down, on more
than one occasion, because they're kids and I shouldn't be
so serious. I'd politely remind him that someone has to win
the game and continue rooting for my son. We'd read them
their favorite book every night. Have monthly picnics in the
park. On our weekly movie night, we'd project our chosen
film and have all the bells and whistles to go along with it.
They'd know the importance of vinyl and be introduced
to the greatest musicians—Billie Holiday, Jackie Wilson,
Marvin Gaye, Prince, Michael Jackson, Aretha Franklin,
Whitney Houston.

Most important, we'd love them. Listen to them. Show
them that you don't have to argue or curse someone out to
get your point across. Show them what love and respect look
like between a man and woman. Hug them and show them
affection so that they're comfortable receiving and reciprocating it. Teach them that it's okay to express themselves and
show emotion. That there's value in vulnerability and effective communication. That although words mean something,
action is more important. So that by the time they're teenagers buzzing with curiosity, Josiah will know he isn't a threat
despite what the world thinks. He won't be a fuckboy who

leads girls on because he doesn't know what he wants or isn't ready and can't communicate. Josie girl will know her value isn't determined by how she meets the needs of others. She won't settle for struggle-love and will know when to walk away from what she doesn't deserve. She will know that as a Black woman, she is beautiful and her only competition. Our young adults will know that while love is beautiful, we humans can make a mess of it, which is why we have to be understanding. However, they will know the value of not losing themselves within that empathy. They will know that at the end of the day, they have to hold themselves accountable and love themselves before they try to love someone else.

Jill Scott's "A Long Walk" was floating through our home's surround-sound speakers when Nicholi called me downstairs. The dining room was picturesque, with candles and vases filled with white and red roses strewn about.

"Tonight, I want you to enjoy yourself and relax. No stressing about anything or anyone."

He filled our glasses with champagne and raised his. "To the most beautiful woman in the world. You've already won this case, and you'll make an exceptional partner, babe. You are my lighthouse."

"And you're my compass."

The Isley Brothers' "Don't Say Goodnight (It's Time for Love)" drifted through the air, just as we drifted into each other's arms. There was no talking; just the rhythmic sounds of the music playing. We stayed like that for a while, holding each other close. Our shadows bouncing gracefully off the walls in the luminous candlelight. The only sounds were the soft melody of the music and our breath crashing gently against each other. As I gazed into my husband' eyes, I found solace. Nicholi returned my gaze, piercing my heart with an abundance of love. Our eyes locked, lips met, and tongues danced with such a fierce passion that time stood still. Bodies wound around each other, clinging together like magnets. Our bedroom was filled with even more candles, and the rose petals scattered about our California king-sized bed added splashes of red to the scene. Our bedside table held a bottle of cognac and whipped cream. As if on cue, Jamie Foxx's "Slow" sauntered into the room.

I eyed him mischievously. "So, this is the last course?"

His hands traveled the length of my spine, sending chills through me. My legs wrapped around his waist, lips desperately searching for his, as we fell in bed. My eyes couldn't be torn away as he stripped. It was like watching Van Gogh paint. I couldn't help it. My husband was beautiful. His chocolate body had muscles in all the right places. Those brown eyes engulfed me, saying *be prepared for a long night.* I was ready to partake in any activity my husband desired. Standing there in all his glory, I wondered if God had created anyone more beautiful than him.

"Faith, wake up. You got to see this."

Faith sat up rubbing her eyes. The clock next to her said it was four in the morning. "What is it, Granny?"

"Your mother." She twisted the wedding ring on her finger. "I don't know what to do no more."

Faith got out of the bed reluctantly. After twenty-one years of experience with her mother, she really didn't want to see what she was doing this early in the morning.

"Go look in the living room." Granny sat on the bed as if she'd never move again. Although it was less than five feet from the bed to the living room, Faith felt as if she was embarking on the longest journey of her life. Her feet felt like they were trying to walk through cement, while her palms were as moist as a criminal waiting to be sentenced in court. Granny trailed her slowly, as if she couldn't bear to see again what she had already witnessed.

Faith heard noises but could barely see. The living room was pitch black. However, the kitchen stove light cast a silhouette near the stairs. Faith stepped closer, seeing what had to be her mother, writhing and moaning a sound she had never heard in the middle of the living room, something between pleasure and agony. Faith plopped herself down on the stairs. She had seen her mother high many times before, but never like this. Naked, she scratched all over her body and rocked from side to side, voicing incoherent, vague utterances.

"Catherine, get up." Granny walked past her toward the bathroom. "You've got to go."

Faith sat in defeat. "Cat, get up." She made no movement at all, except what she had been doing. Faith shook her. "Get up, lady. Get up."

Her mother sat up abruptly. She looked around, her eyes narrowing. "What's going on?" She saw that she was naked and was embarrassed. "How did I get naked in the middle of the floor?" She grabbed for the pile of clothes on a nearby chair. She looked up to see Granny glaring down upon her. "I'm so sorry, Ma. It won't happen again." Her face was ashen as she dressed quickly. "I fell asleep, but I coulda sworn I was on the couch."

"Catherine, I'm tired." Granny's voice trembled. "You got to go."

"Why I gotta go? Cause I fell asleep on the floor? I said I was sorry." She tried protesting further, but Granny wasn't hearing it.

"You were high!" She held her daughter's purse. *"I found that stuff all over the bathroom. It's kids here. You gotta go. I don't wanna hear nothing else."*

Catherine finally noticed her daughter sitting on the stairs. *"Faith,"* she approached her frantically, *"look at my arms, they dried up. Tell her I ain't high."*

Faith tried to keep her eyes off the many dark marks, bruises, and bulging veins.

"It's five in the morning, girl." Terrell came into the house fussing. No one had to ask what he was doing out so late. Everyone knew he was doing the things he loved most: hanging with his friends and drinking. *"Mama said get your stuff, so you can get up outta here. People tired of seeing you like this. You embarrassing your kids."*

"Motherfucker, you don't know nothing." Catherine said with wild eyes. *"I don't embarrass them."* She scratched her neck and arms.

Faith moved to the living room table. The shit had really just hit the fan, as her uncle and mother did not know when to stop arguing.

"You embarrass all of us. I hear about what you do in the streets."

"Fuck you." You could see the veins in her neck throbbing as she climbed the stairs to her room. *"You don't know nothing."*

"Fuck your ugly ass," he spat with venom. *"You need to get some help cause you look horrible."* Terrell retreated into his room and slammed the door.

Faith heard her mother crying.

"*You think I like looking like this,*" she yelled from the top of the stairs. "*I know how I look. That's why I don't look in the mirror. And I don›t embarrass my kids, you embarrass yours, deadbeat bitch.*"

Faith pouted at the table, unsure of which emotion to express: pain, sadness, anger, or empathy. So she just listened.

"*Can't even come in this house and get love from your own family. That's why I stay in the streets.*" Catherine chuckled and then cried harder. Her rapid footsteps back and forth let Faith know she was also unsure of what to do. "*I walk the streets crying every day cause nobody love me. Nobody support me. I do what I gotta do so I can survive. I don't like it, but I got to. Sometimes I'm worth ten dollars, fifteen. On a good day twenty or twenty-five.*"

The door slammed. Faith sat in the darkness and let the tears fall down her face.

My cell shivered on the oak nightstand. I rubbed my eyes, blinking wildly at the clock on my bedside table. It was nearly four in the morning. The caller ID said it was Pat, so it was almost three her time in Chicago.

"Hello?"

Her voice was strained. "It's Granny."

CHAPTER 3
THE FAR SOUTH SIDE
OF CHICAGO

don't like hospitals. In high school, my family had quite a
number of family deaths, including my aunt Whitney, my
grandparents' eldest child. Walking through these white
hallways now reminded me of visiting her. After her death—
and the several that followed over the next seven years—the
thought of returning to a hospital loomed over me like a
shadow of what it ultimately led to: death. My nose wrinkled at the smell of sorrow, pain, and sterilization. Hope and
somberness bounced off the walls like a game of Ping-Pong.
Just as that warm, fleeting feeling leaves, anxiety comes back
even harder.

316. I stood just inside Granny's room door, looking at
her through stinging eyes. Her face and hands were swollen,
tubes and IVs everywhere. She was unrecognizable. A stark
difference from the warmth she typically radiated, with her
glistening eyes. She was always a tireless supporter. In the

fourth grade, I loved the saxophone but was told my hands were too small to play it. Instead, I was given a flute. When it came time to buy it, Cat didn't come through. So I did what any child would do in the situation: called my Granny. Not long after, my mother gave me the money. But she didn't forget to berate me either.

"If you ever come between my mama and me again I'ma beat your ass," she threatened before I left for school one morning.

I didn't understand what I had done wrong. All I knew was that she was angry with me. The silver lining, however, was that Granny kept an exceptional track record of support following that event. Throughout my life she has been an unmovable force as well as a provider of gems that are always delivered on time. Once, in my midtwenties, I was home for someone's birthday party. The party was winding down, yet the house was still filled with many in our large family. It was early morning, and the liquor was taking its toll on everyone. Keyshia Cole's "I Remember" played on the stereo, and halfway through the song Granny started crying. I'd noticed for years now that she'd cry whenever she heard it. When I asked what brought her to tears, she pointed to the stereo on the other side of the room.

"You came home from school and wept with this album on repeat right there," she said wiping at her eyes. "I ain't know what to say to make you feel better. All I knew was you just had to get to the other side of that feeling. I sat on my bed and cried with you."

That shit rocked me. And further solidified my loyalty to her.

By midmorning the hospital's waiting room had turned into a family reunion. There were many people I hadn't seen since my last visit. After graduating from college, I decided I would only come back when necessary. That's how much drama ensued in my family growing up. My grandparents had five kids. Whitney, the oldest, had a vibrant personality with an even bigger smile. She passed when I was a sophomore in high school. Chase had a dramatic and irresistible aura. Women loved him for his charm despite his refusal to hear anyone else's voice but his own. Randy was dark chocolate and only spoke when he had something to say. Terrell never took anything too seriously, not even his newly minted fiancée, according to some family. My mother, Catherine, or Cat as she was called, was the baby of the Moore family. She had a big heart and good intentions that just never seemed to come to fruition. Beyond that, everything and everyone was the same at home. Cousin Shanice, Whitney's daughter, was still devoted to her babies' father, Took, but Took was only devoted to himself. Great Auntie Shirley, one of two of Granny's living siblings, and my favorite, was sweet until she wasn't.

"Good to see you, baby," she said, scooping me into her arms. "When my dancin' buddy gettin' here?"

One thing for certain is that the Moore family had a sense of humor. We cracked jokes and could relate a song lyric or movie line to any conversation. Honestly, it was all good with my family—until it wasn't.

"Girl, be nice." I swear Pat could read my mind. Most people thought she was the big sister because she was taller than me. Pat was, however, the girly girl. From a very early age, she loved doing hair and makeup. So much so that she would terrorize my Barbie dolls by cutting their hair and making them new clothes. It all paid off as she opened her salon, Beauty Marks, a couple of years ago.

"What up, Faye."

There was only one person who called me that. Eli, our sixteen-year-old little brother, who wasn't so little anymore. He stood about 6 feet tall now, and was dressed like the rest of the boys wearing skinny jeans and too small T-shirts. He was damn near a man, but still had a boyish charm about him, and those gorgeous dimples. I stepped back to get a good look at him. He was handsome. He wrapped his arms around me.

"How long you gonna be here this time?"

Pat nudged him in the ribs. "Right. Cause we need to have a talk with him about school and his disappearing acts."

I had known for some time now that Eli was having behavioral problems in school. I didn't know, however, that the boy was ditching. He looked everywhere else but me. I started to ask if he had talked to his mother when my adorable and very spoiled five-year-old niece, Hope, grabbed ahold of my leg and wouldn't let go. I hugged my brother-in-law, Greg, before scooping her up.

"Have you been good, pooh?" We hugged each other as tight as we could. Hope had the uncanny ability to make my heart feel as though it was bursting.

"Yes, Tee Tee."

"Nice! We're all gonna spend some time together before I leave, okay?"

"Books?" She asked with pleading eyes.

"I ain't know people still read books," a husky voice said.

The only person who had a voice like that in this family was Terrell. I turned to see he was still tall as hell, with a shiny, bald head. Trailing not too far behind him had to be his fiancé

Brenda. Her brown weave flowed down her back like a horse's tail; her walk signified that she was proud to be on the arm of her man.

"You'd be surprised at the things people do for enjoyment," I said as my uncle and I half-hugged each other.

"You must be Faith. Your uncle told me all about you and your little job." Brenda said.

I started to tell her that being a defense lawyer was a career, but Pat's elbow stopped me. I swear she had telepathy.

"Still got that long, pretty hair everybody talk about," Brenda said throwing her horse ponytail over her shoulder. "You sure that's all you?"

"Every inch." Brenda brushed my extended hand aside and bear-hugged me. My reflex wanted to push her off, but I thought of Granny and how she always told me to be nice. "And congrats on your engagement. I heard the party was something."

"Thanks. We'll take a nice gift though. You definitely look like you got it."

I chuckled at her little comment. Before I could respond, Pat nudged me in the side again. And then the doctor walked in. He reminded me of *Grey's Anatomy*'s McSteamy: dark wavy locks, bright blue eyes. The way the family stood at attention, you would've thought he was a sergeant.

"I'm Dr. Eric Porter. Frances has had a severe stroke that has paralyzed the left side of her body. She will need both speech and physical therapy."

Stifled groans and sobs filled the waiting room.

"This won't be an easy journey for her, but with the proper support and therapy she can recover," he continued. "Also, her emergency contact is her late husband Charles, so we'll need to update that."

"Put me down." Terrell approached Dr. Porter cooler than the other side of a pillow.

Aunt Shirley cleared her throat. "Now, hold on. How you just gonna do that? You not her only child. What about your siblings, honey? They might wanna help."

Terrell looked amused. "Cat and Chase ain't here. And Randy ain't capable of making no decisions."

Randy, a couple inches shorter than his brother, looked at him like he was crazy. "Yes, I am. But I don't wanna do it."

"Well, I think Faith should help." Aunt Shirley interjected. "Y'all know that education she got help her understand what the people be talking about and stuff."

"Faith a big-time lawyer, so she probably ain't interested. "What you think, Faith?"

The room was so silent you could hear a pin drop.

"Terrell can be the contact. I'll help out wherever else I'm asked."

CHAPTER 4
HARD FACTS

My grandmother has always been the definition of unconditional love to me. Since I was a little kid, I remember her turning the other cheek no matter what was done to her. I've heard grandkids curse her name to hell and even steal the crumbs off her plate while watching her children treat her as if she was their child. Granny has always had a long memory, but a heart of gold. I've heard her express heartache over egregious acts committed against her. I've witnessed her beautiful face washed over in tears with heartbreak. Despite these things, her arms have remained open. She is always present. Always willing. Always available to save the day. Whether she keeps a record or not, I don't know.

But it's the pain behind her shining eyes that resonates with me the most. For years the woman has put herself on the bottom of the totem pole to ensure everyone else stayed on top. I know she's been tired. Tired of being a crutch. Tired of being used and taken advantage of. Tired of being treated as though she doesn't deserve effort from all of us. Tired of tending to flowers that should've bloomed a long, long time ago.

There's something heart-wrenching about seeing a person you love defeated. It's maddening, actually. Unfortunately, I'd seen that look a few months before, when I talked with Granny on FaceTime. She was sitting in the door of her garage sipping a cold brew—a rare occasion—which meant her isolation was serious. She didn't want to be bothered. She stayed cool in the smoldering heat of the summer by dabbing her glimmering forehead with a face towel. Barry White played on the jukebox, reminding us to practice what we preach. With heavy bags under her eyes, they didn't shine as brightly as they normally would. And, for the first time, her smile didn't welcome mine to join.

"I can't keep waiting for these grown people to get they stuff together no more," she said. "I need to get my own place."

"Whatever you need, I'm here. Even if you want a change of scenery and move out of state. You can come live with me and Nicholi, baby."

She chuckled. "I ain't gonna ruin y'all's privacy. But I'll come for a visit and see what it's like. I've got to do something," she pounded her fist on her knee. "I'm ready to be in my own space again. Have my peace of mind. So I don't have to be bothered by nobody, especially people who don't help me."

I flashed my best smile. "That's understandable. You deserve that, baby."

She took a swig of her brew. "When Shanice ain't running behind Took, she remembers me and does what she can. Randy brings me a few dollars every now and then. When your mama in her right mind, she good. Chase gets on my damn nerves and I'm glad Terrell finally moved out." Her eyes clouded. She took another swig, keeping the downpour at bay. "I don't know where I went wrong with them."

It's amazing the things we take for granted when they're not directly impacting us. Peace of mind, our personal space, the things we work hard for. I tried to gauge how I'd feel if there were adults in my home that barely paid rent and rarely contributed to the household. How I'd feel if I had to not only lock my valuables in a safe, but also my towels, tissue, food, and other minuscule items in my bedroom. How I'd react to a person patronizing me like a child in my own home. I couldn't imagine it. And here my Granny was expressing how it did not behoove the people living with her—her very own off-spring and theirs—to contribute more than negative energy. With her heart of gold, it must have pained her. However, finally she accepted, like I had for years now, that she needed to make a change if she was to save herself.

You could tell the liquor was taking effect as Terrell swayed a bit. He stood in the middle of his mother's quaint home addressing his siblings, Aunt Shirley, me, and the rest of his nieces and nephews. His childhood friend, Spider, sat in the background, observing like he has always done since I can remember. The great-grandchildren let their imaginations fly on the tattered brown stairs. My watch said we'd been here for two hours. This meeting ran long for no other reason than people arriving late and then blaming everyone else but themselves for Granny's unfortunate situation. Accountability has never been my family's strong suit.

"Everybody agree we should keep paying Mama bills until she get home," Terrell announced. "I'ma get on that tomorrow since I got her purse. Mama like paying her bills on time and we gonna keep it that way."

Chairs scrapped the worn green carpet as everyone scattered. Most gathered their belongings to leave. Pat shot me a concerned look from the kitchen.

"You really think this gonna work?"

"I think we need to let them do what they say they'll do. This time could be different, Pat."

When Granddaddy Charles died, it was a huge shock for the family because Granny had recently come home from the hospital. She had had a severe heart attack and had to have a pacemaker placed in her chest to regulate her abnormal heart rhythms. I remember the family being in such dissent about her care, but mainly about her life insurance policy because Granddaddy was the beneficiary. I'm not sure why anyone had qualms about him having that role; he was her husband, after all. But I often pondered why they thought they would be a better fit. Would they honor her wishes? Would they give her a lavish funeral or skimp as much as possible to line their pockets with her insurance money? I was only fifteen, so I was kept in the dark. But I knew one thing: it was hard to imagine people honoring a loved one in death when they didn't honor them when they were alive.

Despite the drama that ensued, Granddaddy was at the hospital every day doing whatever was required of him. It's like he nursed Granny back to health himself. Granddaddy Charles was a no-nonsense man who loved his wife. It wasn't surprising because that's all I had ever seen growing up. He catered to his wife. He not only drove her everywhere, but also cooked, ensured everyone gave her her due, and helped maintain the household. Granny finally came home a few weeks before her birthday, on which we gave a surprise party she never wanted. That night I remember Granddaddy and Granny danced all night long. He kept kissing her forehead and she held on to him like I had never seen before. All of us cousins were sound asleep upstairs when Shanice burst into the room, hysterical the following morning screaming he had passed away. We didn't believe it. I remember descending the cold, metal back hallway stairs to see if it was true. Granny's siblings were sitting at the living room table, sullen. Aunt Shirley's eyes were bloodshot. I looked to Granny for confirmation. Her blank stare broke me. Granddaddy Charles had passed in bed next to her while they slept. The queen no longer had her knight in shining armor or his protection.

Spider made his way into the kitchen and stood too close for comfort. True to his name, he was creepy, ugly, and oftentimes had to be reminded to keep his hands to himself. He was one of my uncle Terrell's longtime friends. As my sister, cousins, and I grew up, his eyes were ever watchful. Always commenting on how we looked, jokingly of course, and bragging about the amount of what I believed to be imaginary money he had. I couldn't take a man seriously who constantly eyed and hit on young girls, let alone his so-called best friends' nieces. Even before we were legal, his thoughts were loud and clear. In undergrad, I came home for another surprise party for Granny. I saw the twinkle in his eyes when I danced. He joined and the chorus of laughter and applause took off. It was a good old spectacle for the family. Per usual, no one thought anything of it. That's just good old Spider being silly, drunk, and loving the music.

"Get him, girl," Aunt Shirley shouted. "Show him what you got."

I really didn't want to show him. However, I continued to make myself uncomfortable to keep them comfortable. He damn sure let me know how he felt when he pressed his manhood against me as I half-hugged him at the end of the song. "I miss your scent, girl," he whispered in my ear. "I gotta couple dollars for you if you wanna hang out."

In that moment I wanted to rip his fucking balls off. But doing so would mean I'd have to speak the words I've never wanted to see the light of day. Our uncles never stopped him or his advances. It's funny how the people who are supposed to protect you always leave the door open for harm.

"You still married, Faith?" Spider's eyes roamed my body like a map. He tried to slip an arm around me but I dodged him like Neo.

"Yes, I'm well satiated."

"What that mean?"

"My husband keeps me full."

He licked his severely chapped lips. "You always had a way with them big words. It's good seeing you."

"Mmm hmm."

Shanice threw her head back in laughter. "That nigga ain't never gonna change and you either, Faith." She took a sip from her red plastic cup and frowned at the taste of the liquor. She was still beautiful. She eyed the door while checking her watch.

"Waiting for Took to show?" I see y'all still going strong."

"Still going strong upside her motherfucking head," Aunt Shirley said. "You need to leave his ass alone. He ain't shit."

"He trying, aight."

"Tryna what? Ruin your life one day at a time?" That tickled Aunt Shirley pink. Pat and I tried not to laugh. We weren't successful.

"You know what? I'm gone. Monroe, Junior," Shanice stormed out of the kitchen, "let's go."

"What? He ain't shit. She can do better."

It was no secret that Shanice's relationship wasn't #relationshipgoals, but she loved him. So, we all knew she would stay until she reached her breaking point. I just hope she isn't broken beyond repair once it's over.

"I treat my lady like a lady," Eli smiled his boyish grin, "that's what my sisters taught me."

"That's right baby," Aunt Shirley high-fived him. "'Cause I know you smooth with the ladies. You so handsome, boy."

"He ain't too smooth with school, though." Pat was unimpressed. "What we teach you about that?"

He sighed, pulling his baggy pants up, a sure sign that this conversation wasn't what he signed up for. "College ain't for me."

"So, what's for you? Standing on the corner with your little friends?"

"We be out there trying to figure it all out," Eli explained. "You gotta trust the process."

"You can only trust the process when you have a plan and you're actively following it," I said. "We know college isn't for everyone, but you can also get a trade like plumbing or drive trucks."

He scoffed. "I ain't interested in that."

"Cause it sound like work," Pat said. "I guess you'll figure it out when you get tired of them streets."

"Mmm hmm," Aunt Shirley agreed. "And there ain't nothing nice about them either."

CHAPTER 5
CATCHING UP

Rain pounded against the house like a madman at the door. Faith gazed out of the living room window. The overcast sky was platinum gray. Not welcoming at all. She buttoned her coat just thinking about the chill that awaited her once she ventured outside.

"We'll leave as soon as Granny heads out," she told Kent. They were both home for fall break and wanted to spend as much time together as they could before Faith returned to Tennessee to finish out her freshman year.

Faith watched her mother fix something to eat in the kitchen. She had popped up a few days ago. Granny let her stay to her siblings' disbelief and anger. She was only refueling, Faith thought. Then she'd disappear for several weeks again. Eli ran from the back room and right into Faith's arms. She squeezed him tight. He was only four years old. Faith wanted to take him to college with her, but Granny insisted she leave him and focus on her studies.

"Stop running through here, Eli," Cat shouted as she slammed the refrigerator shut.

Faith squeezed her little brother's cheeks. He had the cutest dimples, and she couldn't get enough of his little high-pitched laugh. "Are you ready for bed?" She tickled him so good he could barely answer.

"Yes. I brush my teeth. See?" He opened his mouth wide, displaying two front teeth missing.

Faith fake-inspected his mouth, then crinkled her nose. "It doesn't smell like you did." Eli burst with laughter as Faith tickled him more.

"All right, all right," Patience joined in the tickling of her little brother. "I think it's time we get you in bed."

Eli's almond-shaped eyes began to water, his little mouth quivering. "Hey," Patience caressed his cheeks, "tomorrow me, you, and Faith are gonna spend the whole day at Chuck E. Cheese. If you go to sleep, tomorrow will be here sooner."

He jumped out of Pat's arms and ran to the back room. "Goodnight to you, too," Faith called after him. "I'll be up early in the morning, so whatever time you're ready we can leave, Pat."

Her baby sister played with a strand of her purple hair. "Good, because Eli gonna wake up before you. I'll be ready." She followed Eli. "Good night."

Granny came out of her room zipping up her jacket. "Faith, can you please look underneath the bed for my other boot? Shirley outside."

Faith went and looked underneath her bed. She found the other boot, and also brought out her grandmother's keys, cell phone, and purse. "You don't want to forget these things either, lady."

She zipped up her boot and put the rest of the things in her purse. "Thanks, baby. Catherine," Granny called. "Are you ready? I'm about to go."

Catherine came out of the kitchen chewing a sandwich. "Ready for what?"

"I'm about to leave, so you need to leave."

"I have to leave? Are you serious?" She looked around the room confused.

Granny drummed her fingers on the table. "Yes. I'm sorry, but you gotta go. You can come back tomorrow."

Faith sat on the stairs next to her boyfriend. He rubbed her hand, while she bounced her foot.

"Where am I supposed to go, Mama?"

"You have to go, Catherine. Now come on, Shirley's waiting."

Granny stood at the door with her things. Catherine turned and mumbled underneath her breath. She wrapped up her sandwich and put it in a plastic bag along with some more food. She slammed the cupboards as she moved then stomped up the stairs, stepping over Faith and her boyfriend. They heard her rummaging through the drawers right before she returned downstairs with her coat and shoes on.

"I can't believe this shit." She stalked out the door.

Granny looked at Faith. "I'll be back in a few hours."

"All right."

Faith watched her mother in the heavy rain as she buckled her seatbelt. "Can we drop Cat off somewhere first, please?"

Kent pulled up beside Catherine, rolling his window down. It was pouring cats and dogs.

"Cat, get in. We'll take you wherever you need to go."

Her mother splashed angrily through the large puddles she walked through. Faith couldn't tell if it was rain or tears streaming down her face.

"I don't need anyone. Go ahead."

He looked at Faith. She nodded and he drove off. Faith watched her mother in the rearview mirror. A pained stare. She silently prayed that her mother would be able to stay somewhere safe and warm for the night. That she'd live to see the next day. That she'd give up the drugs and come home for good. Where she belonged. Amen.

If Granny's eyes shined any brighter we'd all have to wear sunglasses to look at her. It was only a couple of days later, but as soon as the doctors said it was okay for the family to visit, we did. She'd be starting therapy soon to learn to walk again and regain use of her left arm. She hadn't been able to move it since she woke. Dr. Porter said she might not have full recovery of it.

"When I come home, I'll need everybody help. Y'all gonna be there for me, right?"

"Of course we are, baby." Shanice gave her a kiss on the forehead. "You might as well call me your nurse because I'ma be there for whatever you need."

I hadn't seen Granny look this restful in years. Her honey-brown skin was back to its normal radiant glow. Her grayish white hair, always in a short cut, had gotten its soft curls back. And even without teeth, she had the most beautiful smile. Despite the situation, I was glad she was finally getting the rest and care she deserved. Things could only get better from here.

"Here you go, lady." I handed her a new Chapstick. She hated dry lips and taught me the same.

"Thanks, little lady." She put quite a bit of the balm on her parched lips. "Oh, that feels great. My lips been looking like a wrinkled napkin around here. So how long you staying? I bet not too long, huh?" She tried to laugh it off but failed.

"I'm leaving next week. I have that new case in L.A., so I have to travel. I'm hoping it won't be too long of a trial."

The O'Jays played in the background of joyous banter.

"I want you here with me for a little while longer," she said, squeezing my hands tight, "but I'll take what I can get."

Damn. I wanted to tell her there is no place I'd rather be. However, I knew that would mean nothing when I left. I was going where I wanted to be. If I won—pardon me, when I won—this case, I'd fulfill my childhood dream. My client is being charged with murder; I've read everything in the brief and beyond. My gut tells me he didn't do it, and my gut is rarely wrong. This is my case. I can feel it. Still, I was torn. It felt bad to chase my dreams while Granny endured a tough time.

She motioned for me to come closer. "Before you leave, I need you to do me a favor."

Eli's golden-brown skin glistened in the sunlight. He was beautiful. He had the same enchanting almond-shaped eyes as Cat and Pat, long eyelashes, and the cutest dimples that made you squeeze his cheeks. Sixteen years later, Eli had gone from the world's best baby (in my book) to a young man. I had always wondered how our lives would be at this time. Sixteen years ago, it wasn't the best. At the time, I was a sophomore in high school and Pat was in sixth grade. It was a tense time. My family fought a lot. Everyone's tongue was razor sharp and no one cared how much blood they spilled. I remember when Cat told me she was pregnant. She was sitting at the living room table smoking a cigarette. Her sweatpants were bright blue and the tattered gray T-shirt she wore hung loose over a small yet pronounced belly bump. I knew what it was before she even opened her mouth.

"I'm pregnant. He'll be here in a few weeks."

I was fucking livid. How could she be so careless? Things were more than hard enough. She was still doing her disappearing acts, but Pat and I knew how to manage those now. However, this new baby would need someone to take care of it. How much did diapers, wipes, and baby food cost? He needed a crib and we didn't have any extra room. A car seat and clothes for the ride home. He would need someone present. Someone who quelled his cries when he needed to be fed, changed, or wanted attention.

I didn't know how to care for a baby. When Eli was born, I learned quickly. I was sixteen. Trying to reach my goal of getting out. At the time, I wasn't inspired by anyone in my family. I didn't want my siblings, and any other cousin who came behind me, looking at me with disappointing eyes. If I could get out and go to college, sixteen years from now I could make a difference. My siblings wouldn't need to ask anyone for help. We could escape the mundane life our family was content with. We could be better humans.

I was sixteen. Plotting how to provide a better life for a child that wasn't even mine.

"We been having these talks with you for a long time now. We always tell you that you have two sisters who will basically do anything for you. But what we always say you gotta do?"

"Be good and go to school and get good grades."

I've always enjoyed Pat's taking lead on these conversations with Eli. People have always commented on my calm demeanor, but Pat's was next-level. We were having a picnic at the local park. Bright green leaves rustled in the breeze, while children's joyful laughter ricocheted off the playground. Hope played freely, and constantly beckoned us to watch her go down the slide.

"We always said you can talk to us, too. What's going on?" Eli picked at the checkered blanket. "I don't like school. It's too long. The teachers ask too many questions, and somebody always gotta say something to me. Them fights don't even be my fault."

"You gotta learn how to tune out the bullshit. People always gonna have something to say. Ain't that right, Faith?"

"Absolutely. Let them talk. It's easier said than done, but you'll benefit in the end."

"But I ain't no punk."

"No one said you were. And if someone does, you don't have anything to prove. There's power in choosing inaction," I said.

The look on his face said he doubted that. "I been thinking about Mama, too. Just wanna make sure she come home."

"Your mother ain't never gonna change," Pat chuckled.

Pat has always been the sensitive one when it came to our mother. Well, at least until Eli became old enough to understand what was happening around him. I always tried to understand why my mother chose to indulge her lifestyle for years. I never wanted Cat to live the street life, but she made it clear a long time ago that that's where she wanted to be. That's why not only Granny, but my siblings meant the world to me. Pat and I knew what it was like to go to bed every night wondering whether our mother would live to see the next day. We knew how it felt to be neglected, despite engaging in any and every activity just to get her to come out and show her support, to see you. Unfortunately, Eli now understood those very same things.

"Well, I hope she do," he said.

"Boy, we been hoping for a long time." Pat shook her head in disbelief as if she couldn't believe what she had just said. "She ain't gonna change unless she want to."

CHAPTER 6
SHATTERED GLASS

"Shanice, you can't leave." Pat was fuming as I peeped out of my bedroom window. "What about Granny?"

Shanice and Took had packed their things. He was loading them into the trunk of his rusted vehicle. "Pat, it's time we start taking care of ourselves."

Pat looked as if she wanted to hit her. "You realized that right now? Today? After years living off Granny? What about her? She needs us all now more than ever."

"I love Granny. She been like a mama to me. But Took finally found a job and you know I could use his help paying these bills. And you know Granny is trying to move anyway."

"You know she always say that and don't. This ain't the time to leave her either. You bogus as hell."

Shanice smacked her lips. "Look, we gotta do what's best for us." Took started the engine. It sounded like they wouldn't make it far.

"You a true Moore." Pat backed away from the car. "Always looking out for yourself."

"Keep me posted on Granny. We'll come see her soon."

Down the stairs I went to the kitchen too angry to savor relief of the pot of tea I began brewing. I thought of my selfish family members. How could they leave Granny's side during this horrible time? One thing's for certain: if the roles were reversed, you would have to fight our grandmother to think of herself. Pat sat at the kitchen table devoid of her usual astuteness. I placed teacups and saucers for both of us. She remained mute.

"I know you likely want to say 'I told you so,' but I knew this would happen. Not this soon, but eventually."

I grabbed the ginger, honey, and sugar out of the corner cabinet and lemons from the fridge. "Do you want toast or croissants?" She didn't answer, but always preferred croissants. "Don't fret. I'm going to pay Granny's rent for the remainder of her lease. Just to make sure at least that's taken care of."

Pat, hands tightening, raised her head. "Just because you throw your money around to solve problems don't make it right, Faith."

"So, your car doesn't count?"

"I told you I'm gonna pay you back."

"That was two years ago."

Pat stood abruptly, spilling her tea. "Don't trip. I'ma get you your money ASAP." She stalked out of the kitchen, fuming.

Honestly, I didn't care that she hadn't paid me back. I knew she was going to take her time. Most important, I knew the bond I now shared with my sister was still maturing. It wasn't that long ago when we only shared brief hugs and even shorter conversations. I was so used to acting like her mother,

I didn't know how to be Pat's big sister. It didn't help that I was also emotionally unavailable. It didn't help that while I was fighting for our mother's love, I was too blind to see my little sister was doing the same for me. We started cultivating our relationship when I was in my midtwenties. Sharing our stories of strife and triumph with Cat. Pat made me come to grips with the fact that my leaving impacted her more than I had thought. My leaving was to force Cat's hand, get her to be more responsible. All it did was shift the load from me to Pat.

Granddaddy Charles and Granny let me move in when I was sixteen. It was only a few months after Eli was born. If you ask my mother today why I left, she'll tell you it's because I didn't want to clean. I left because I was tired of seeing random men revolving in and out of the house. I left because half of my life I'd watched my mother being abused. I left because I was tired of seeing her self-sabotage. I was tired of her disappearing acts. It started as just for a few hours, then it became overnight, then grew to days, then weeks and months. She'd return as if she had only gone to the grocery store. The more she disappeared, the more I did, too. After Eli was born, I was juggling him, school, dance, and trying to keep the house in order. I guess I always thought Pat was good. It never crossed my mind that she might need me. Shit, was I wrong.

"I just thought you ain't like me," she told me one night on the phone. "You danced, so I danced, too. I even tried to write poetry like you."

It still hurts me to my core to know that Pat always wanted me to notice her and I never saw her. Once I got out, my plan was to always be a positive influence and be a good example for my siblings. I'm glad Pat saw me. I didn't give her the love she deserved and needed, but at least I left her footprints to follow. Cat always told us that we were all we had.

"If I leave this earth today, y'all have each other," she'd say. "It's just you and your brother and sister. Treat each other right—and don't let no one come between y'all. Don't be like me and my siblings."

Sibling relationships are delicate. Oftentimes they are not handled with care. You know each other's true colors and intentions. You know the foulest things to say when hitting below the belt, and when to strike. Sibling relationships are your first introduction to love, reciprocity, and consent, but also to jealousy, insecurity, and hatred. What a beautiful yet ugly web we weave.

"I will definitely be picking you up from the airport tomorrow night. You need me to bring anything, baby?"

"No, thanks. All I need is you."

Nicholi's concerned eyes were loud as we FaceTimed. "Your thoughts have been somewhere else this whole call. What's on your mind?"

"Nothing really. Just Granny and all this shit here. And this case."

"You know you can only do what you can. Just stick to the mission."

"I'm trying to figure that out."

The squeaky creak of the door opening diverted our attention.

"I'll call you back, babe."

My mother was only a few inches taller than me, at 5 foot 6, but we had the same full lips and brown eyes. All her kids did. Per usual, her hair was cut short like Angela Bassett's in

Waiting to Exhale, and she had the same infectious smile as her mother.

"Hey, Cat."

I wanted to get up to hug her, but my feet wouldn't move. She and I never really had a physical relationship. I could count on one hand how many times she'd hugged me. Growing up, it just became a custom for us not to embrace.

When I was nine years old, her boyfriend Michael died. It was late one evening; Pat and I were sleeping when we were startled awake by glass shattering and anguished cries. I told Pat to stay in bed and rushed downstairs, only stopping when I saw Cat at her wit's end. When I asked what was wrong, she told me to go back to bed. I can still hear her cries 'til this day.

She, life, was never the same after that. Before, she was always happy. Hell, we all were. I don't remember any embraces or activities, but it's the last time I remember my mother being genuinely happy and our lives stress free.

Overnight I went from a child to a woman. Not long after, that night, substance abuse and men became my mother's primary focus. Late nights turned into early mornings waiting for her return home. For years I watched Cat be abused mentally, physically, and emotionally. In turn, she abused me. The only reciprocity I came to understand.

At times we went without hot water and electricity. Pat and I did our homework by candlelight, then I'd warm pots of water for our baths. Other times, our apartment's front window was typically boarded up from people constantly breaking it. Holidays weren't joyful. Thanksgiving reminded me there was nothing to be thankful for, while Christmas became a constant reminder that anything you ask for can be taken away. After three years of break-ins and having all our presents stolen, I stopped asking for gifts and only looked forward to waking up.

It took me years to realize I had created an invisible force shield, suppressing all my feelings. For the longest time I wouldn't allow myself to feel or love. As a child, any thoughts of being in relationships quickly diminished every time one of those ain't-shit guys raised their hand to her face. My heart resembled what hers looked like: hard, black, ugly, and bruised. I was lost. Confused. But most of all, angry. How could my own mother not show me love and affection? All those things I never got from her, so in turn her motherhood was never up for reelection. Twenty-three years later, she's still my mother and I love her. Twenty-three years later, I could at least make an effort.

Move, I thought, forcing my feet out of the cement they were stuck in.

"We were worried about you."

Cat waved me off. I'm pretty sure I got my extreme nonchalance from her.

"You mean your brother and sister?"

"Me, too."

"Faith, I know I ain't been the best mother."

"Cat—"

"I always loved you," she interjected. "You ain't give me no trouble. Ever. And I am so proud of you and your sister because y'all didn't turn out like me."

She'd said that for years now. The first time it was slightly different. We had been living in Harvey for about a year then. For a town intended to be an example for Christian values, the city far south of Chicago was a reminiscent shadow of that proclamation by the time we moved there in 1996. Luckily, I was able to catch glimmers of light by some decent residents.

Like Mr. R., he had a candy store in his basement. When my cousins came over, we'd take off up the street, walk up the gravel alley, and race to the basement door of Mr. R's house. He had all the candy and snacks. But what I remember most about the big-bellied, brown man is that he was always patient. It may seem minuscule, but imagine kids in and out of your candy store and half of the time they don't know what they want. Out of all those years of frequenting his store, I never once saw him upset or rush anyone. He reminded me of Ms. Jackson. She owned the corner store just up the block from our apartment. Ms. Jackson wore black wire-rimmed glasses, always wore her hair down, and barely said more than a few sentences.

When I was eight, Cat started sending me with a note with her permission to buy cigarettes from Ms. Jackson. One day, she sent me with a note and told me to get two cans of tomato paste for the dinner she was making. At the register, I handed Ms. Jackson the note and put the money on the counter. She lazily threw a pack of Newport 100s in a paper bag.

"You don't have enough. Put one can of the tomato paste back."

She handed me the paper bag and watched as I walked down the two-aisle store to put the can back in its place. I kept thinking about how mad Cat would be if I came home with only one can. So, I decided to steal it. I walked to the freezer, looking intently to make her think I wanted a drink. Then I went to the snacks aisle and acted like I couldn't figure out which chips I wanted. When I felt I'd fooled her, I walked back to the can section and dropped it in my bag as I passed. I had one foot out of the door when Ms. Jackson stopped me.

"Just because you can't afford what you need doesn't make it okay to steal, little girl. Put it back."

I've never told anyone about what happened that day for shame, but the lesson has always stuck with me. Just like Okay.

Okay was a formidable man. Yes, his name was Okay. Well, at least that's what we kids thought, because it's all we ever heard him say. Okay was a six foot three, wild-Afro-sporting, milk-chocolate man with a toothless smile. He walked as if he had somewhere to be. I don't remember any of us ever talking about Okay or questioning why he acted the way he did. I mean, it was clear that something was wrong. However, we just assumed it was drugs or alcohol abuse. When I think about him now, I realize he likely had some mental health issues. Okay was an example that you never know what people are going through.

The horizontal brown brick building we lived in had five apartments. We were number one. There was nothing special about it. The only thing between our bland apartment building and a large plot of undeveloped land was an alley. Quite frankly, our building stood out oddly because it was the only one on the block, despite my elementary school's being located directly across the street. One time Cat took Pat and me to the park. Pat was four. I was eight. There were multicolored leaves scattered about on the ground. A crispness to the air too. I remember Cat putting polka-dot gloves on Pat, who sat on the swing encouraging me to push her. Mama sat beside us smoking a cigarette. Her gaze focused on something intangible in front of us. She didn't say anything for the longest time.

"I got a drug problem," she finally said. Pat giggled as she found herself going a bit higher each time I pushed her. "Are you okay?" I was unsure what I was supposed to say. Cat took a long pull on her cigarette. Her eyes telling a story her mouth would never speak. "I will be. But I know one thing," she said, blowing the smoke out of her mouth like a pro. "My kids will be better than me." Whatever that was supposed to mean; I didn't ask. Quite frankly, I never asked anything as we grew older. I never asked why she left Pat and me in the house for hours on end. Never asked what the blackened spoons and pipes that I found around the house were. Never asked why she allowed her boyfriends to abuse her. Never asked if she thought about how her actions affected her kids. Never did I once ask why she chose not to be present for us. I never asked any questions because I thought she would change. I thought one day she would wake up and see that her children were all she needed. Not a toxic man. Not drugs or booze. Not unhealthy relationships. All she needed was us. Period. For years, I tried to figure out why she would rather be numb than be present in the world where her children existed. I'd heard stories about the street life. And it didn't sound appealing to me. Sleeping outside or in abandoned places for days on end. Dirty clothes. The possibility of submitting oneself to heinous subjections to get the drug you can't afford. Being beaten for those very same reasons, or putting your family in harm's way. Those thoughts made me sick to my stomach every time they surfaced. Yet here we were, all these years later. And I still hadn't asked any questions.

"Y'all haven't failed at life." Cat couldn't hold her heartbreak any longer as her grief poured out in a flood of tears. "And I know y'all won't let Eli do it either. Really, I'm proud of y'all for loving y'all selves. That's something that I'm just learning how to do. So if it's 'cause of me that y'all are who y'all are, I'm grateful for that."

I wiped at my stinging eyes, keeping the downpour at bay. My throat was as dry as cotton balls. Tongue felt like sandpaper against the roof of my mouth. Body stiff as cardboard. In these moments I always felt like this. Never knowing truly how to express myself. *Comfort her*, I always tell myself. *Show her you love her.* Instead, I did what I know best: deflect and reassure.

"That was in the past, lady. If we can move on, so can you. We just have to keep moving forward."

My phone buzzed on the dresser. Granny's icon popped up on Facetime. Cat wiped at her tear-stained face. "She doesn't know I'm home. I came straight here."

"It'll be fine," I said. "Hey, lady. I'm bringing you a surprise today." I showed my mother's face in the camera. Granny's eyes lit up like a kid's on Christmas Day.

"Catherine," her free palm slapped her forehead. "It's about time you showed up. Hurry up and get up here 'cause you have to get caught up with my doctors." She put the camera to her mouth, whispering, "I don't think Terrell understands what he says, so you need to get here quick."

CHAPTER 7
NEW DIRECTIONS

"Granny, I don't mind paying the bill. It's only two hundred dollars." Faith filled out a check and handed it to her grandmother. She waved her off and crossed the living room to her favorite recliner.

"I can't take your money. It's bad enough you're working full-time while at school. You been in Tennessee for three years and ain't nobody around here sent you a dime. We should be getting money together to help you."

Faith looked at her grandmother sternly. In that moment she realized that's where she got her stubbornness. "That's okay, lady. I'm getting myself through, and your support is all that matters. Besides, you can't risk the lights being cut off. You've helped me my whole life. This is the least I can do."

Granny seemed to look through her granddaughter. A long sigh escaped her thin lips. "Your uncle and cousins are supposed to give me their portion of the money this morning. Let's see what they do first."

Faith's lips pressed together in a tight grimace. She wanted to note that if they didn't have the money now, they wouldn't have it later. Although she understood why her grandmother had so much hope in them, she didn't understand why it hadn't diminished yet after so many letdowns.

Six hours later, Granny sat in the same spot. Only now she peered sightlessly out the window. The only movement was of her hands wringing around the other.

"Lady, it's almost five o'clock," Faith said. "Let me go ahead and pay the bill so it's taken care of. When they bring you the money, just keep it."

Although her eyes were soft, Granny looked at Faith, defeated. "I'll give the money back to you. Thanks, little lady."

Faith kissed her on the cheek. "I'll be back shortly." In a race against the clock, Faith bounded out the front door and took off on her bike to pay the bill.

"Don't worry, it's all taken care of. I put what you told me to back in your safe." Granny looked as though she didn't believe me. It was my last visit with her before leaving in a few hours. "You want me to give your life insurance policy to someone else? That way someone here can act quickly if I can't be reached?"

"No, hold on to it for me. I know you gonna answer. It was good seeing you, baby," she said, squeezing my hand. "Next time, you got to stay longer, okay?"

"I will, and remember, you can always visit. Anytime."

Heavy footsteps and curse words pierced my ears from the hallway. That could only mean one thing. I stepped outside Granny's room, closing the door behind me.

"Hey, y'all know Granny need to rest."

"Wait a minute, that's my big sister, I know that shit." Aunt Shirley caught her breath before continuing. "I'm walking past the people and they stop me talking about this bald-headed motherfucker ain't been answering his phone. They say Frances insurance only paying for twelve days here and that day is tomorrow."

"I told you ain't nobody call me. All we gotta do is pay the five hundred dollars for her to stay the rest of the month," Terrell said, turning to me. "Could you pay the money and then we'll give it back to you?"

Aunt Shirley snorted. "You know his ass lying, right?"

"I'm tryna get Mama bill paid," Terrell snapped back.

"You tryna be slick motherfucker. I'ma pay my big sister bill. And if y'all don't pay me back, I'm gonna be a problem."

"It won't have to come to all of that," I said. "I'll pay it. Save your money."

"You sure, baby?" Aunt Shirley's doe eyes sparkled. "Yes, don't worry about it."

"Good. 'Cause I ain't have it no way. But I would've found it for my big sister."

I took off to find out where I needed to take care of the bill. As I rounded the corner, I could still hear them going at it.

"Lady, you know you be doing too damn much," Terrell said.

"Says the jackass who can't answer his phone," Shirley shot back. "You can get the hell away from me."

Although I was glad to head home, I wasn't too thrilled to leave. This was such a critical time for Granny, and she needed all the help she could get. People were already turning their backs on her and I didn't want her to put me in the same category. I had to work, which has always been the case.

Work to get to college, then work to stay there and graduate, the same for law school, and now my career. I have a fear of failing, and I've never wanted to fail my Granny.

Litter and loiterers lined the streets as I made my way to the airport. A modern-day Okay gallivanted about singing what had to be his favorite song. Barefoot children with bottoms blacker than coffee grounds ran up and down the street, while Black boys stood on corners like they owned them. It made me wanna holler, just like Marvin Gaye on the car radio. While the feeling was fleeting, the serendipitous weather provided a bit of joy.

Passing the corner store, I saw a face that should've been in school. Eli stood wide-legged with a pint in one hand and the other held a blunt to his lips. He catcalled a young girl walking past whose clothes left little to the imagination. My heart sank. My little brother was the reincarnation of his uncles and cousins. The one thing Pat and I never wanted for him. It's truly unfortunate that we don't have any male role models in the family. No example. No leaders. All Eli had been shown is womanizers who depend on women to take care of them. God forbid they try to actually make something of themselves. God forbid they try to show the young eyes watching them that there is more to life than the circumference of where you grew up. God forbid they try and put effort into something else other than fulfilling their own needs or desires.

I hopped the curb of the store's parking lot.

"Get in the car."

"Faith?" Eli looked surprised. "I thought you was gone."

"Not yet. Let's go."

"I'm hanging with my bros—"

"I'm not gonna tell you again."

He got in the car without a word. I wasn't sure what I could possibly say to make him understand. He already knew what he was doing was wrong. I shook my head in disbelief as we parked in front of the house.

"You ain't have to embarrass me like that in front of my guys," he said slamming the car door.

"That wasn't even close to embarrassing, and don't walk away from me when I'm talking to you."

"Why?" He turned around brazen-faced. "You ain't never around anyway. Just leave. That's what you wanna do anyway."

"Damn." Terrell sat on the porch drinking a beer. "You must've saw him at the corner store, huh?"

"I take it you did? And didn't say anything?"

"That boy gonna do what he want to," he said, taking a quick sip of his beer. "He stay out in them streets, he gonna turn out like Cat."

"What that supposed to mean," Eli stood his ground in front of his uncle, clenching his fist so hard the veins in his knuckles protruded.

"You betta get out my face, boy."

"Don't you ever talk shit about my mama again." Eli barely budged when I tried to move him.

"Just go in the house," I said, finally getting his feet uprooted. He backed away, hate seething from his pores.

"You better listen to your big sister, boy. She got a plane to catch."

My uncle and I locked eyes. "I'm staying now. I need to make a phone call."

CHAPTER 8
SMILING FACES

W hen I was fifteen, my grandparents moved to this house in Riverdale. The city on Chicago's far south side wasn't as picturesque as others with its tree-lined streets scattered with abandoned homes and properties. The park, which was located amidst the corner store, laundromat, and liquor store, was in desperate need of more playground structures. Residents sat on their porches to gossip about the latest antics and watch their children play. Train tracks ran through the lively city, proving to be a nuisance more than anything. Trains would stop and sit for hours or blow their whistles during ungodly hours.

Pass the tracks on 138th and across the bridge heading toward 130th was Altgeld Garden Homes, one of the first Chicago Housing Authority public housing projects. Covering about two hundred acres, the housing project primarily consists of two-story row houses with nearly fifteen hundred units. While Altgeld was built to provide improved housing for Black World War II vets, that got lost in translation somewhere down the line as it became known as Chicago's "toxic donut." The housing project was surrounded not only by rivers and lakes, but also by several landfills and industrials sites, including the Acme Steel Plant and the Pullman factory. To this day, it isn't safe to drink the water or breathe the air, honestly.

My family was no stranger to Altgeld as they were raised there and still resided there when my cousins and I were very young. I remember the back-to-school parades and catching the Chews candy thrown to the crowd. On Sundays we went to the skating rink at Our Lady of the Gardens, formerly a private school within the community. They'd give us one dollar and we felt like we were rich for all that we got—chips, juices, candy, hot dogs. The most fun came during the summer, when we'd go to the field and attend the Old Timer's Picnic. There was nothing but space, opportunity, and countless grills and speakers blasting to keep anyone entertained. My family would arrive early, find our spot in the shade, and set up our lawn chairs. Granddaddy would get the grill going, and Granny played the tunes. When things were settled, my cousins and I would take off, dodging through the thick crowd to explore and find other family and friends. We only returned for food and then, at the end of the day, well after sundown when we knew the adults were ready to leave. While the Gardens has earned a reputation for much strife in the community, I never felt unsafe. Some of my favorite childhood memories happened there.

My grandparents' new, but old, white house had black accents and was huge, with six bedrooms, seven if you counted the basement, and three full baths. My cousins and I believed them rich to be able to afford such a grandiose place.

Nevertheless, we explored the house like the new territory it was. We found the old walkways in the upstairs hallway, occasionally using them as the perfect hiding place for not only people but also anything else our grandparents didn't need to find. Our laughs bounced off of the empty walls as we raced through the house. We'd start at the grass-green carpeted stairs in the living room, then dart upstairs through the top floor of the house, and finally zoom down the metal back hallway stairs.

Hands down the best part of the house was the basement. Granddaddy hung up lights that not only changed colors but also lit up to the sound of music. We made sure those lights were on when we skated around the room too. Other times we'd make up dance routines; our family was the only audience we ever needed.

During the summer we hung clothes outside on the clothing line, attached from the house to the garage, which also made for an intense reenactment of *The Goonies'* final fight scene as the sky changed from powder blue to a beautiful blend of orange, red, and yellow. Granny and family would sit inside the shade of the garage listening to music, while Granddaddy Charles would always be stationed at the grill. It was a sight to see. The thick smoke careening toward the sky. Hearing the sizzle of the hot dogs, hamburgers, and brats. Smelling so delicious I could taste them. Watching Granddaddy master it in his signature blue fedora hat, which he'd take off occasionally to wipe his sweating bald head. When they had a party— and there was always a party—both the backyard and front were filled with family and friends roaming about with either plastic cups filled with beer or Granny's special punch. The recipe was a secret she kept close. Her expertly curated mix led people to a state of euphoria. Anyone who put the elixir to their lips vibrated higher. Happy eyes drooped further after additional indulgences. It felt as if we had been transported to another planet as the house became a carousel of lights, fun, and nonstop action. My cousins and I watched as the adults played pool in the garage, danced like there was no tomorrow in the driveway, and listened in awe as our older cousins had epic rap and singing battles on the front porch. Even the occasional brawl was entertaining, as someone was bound to say the drunken words their sober thoughts would never admit.

My cousins and I would take positions throughout the house—someone would man the basement, backyard, front porch, kitchen, and living room—and we'd report back to each other, giddy with laughter, in complete disbelief of what we had just witnessed. As we grew older, those conversations eventually turned into quick phone calls and text messages where we started talking our own shit. We were no longer surprised when things went down because we knew each person's character. Quite frankly, I loved it.

Granted, it was pure joy watching my family and their friends have a good time. But it was equally exhilarating to see if people had the same energy when the person they talked shit about came around. Would they actually express what they had said earlier? Would they stand by whatever they'd done and not apologize for it? In other words, would shit get real? Just watching those interactions all those years taught me how to perfect my poker face. Taught me how to let things roll off my shoulder in public and keep my emotions on lock.

After moving in, it was amazing to see such a big house become filled with things, like fancy leather furniture. Small animal statues, mostly elephants because Granny believed they were lucky, were strategically placed about. Three large custom-made diamond-shaped mirrors hung on the dining room wall. They cast light from the house's gigantic front window, and caught the actions of its inhabitants and visitors: the shared glances of disapproval, whispers of doubt, and uninvited touches. So much had happened in this house. And the living room was the star of the show. It's where ideas were born and opinions—always believed to be law—shattered dreams, crushed hearts, and killed spirits. Where unabashed apologies thrived. Where people became much more familiar with the floor than the ceiling. All because pride took precedence over progress and accountability. It's truly unfortunate, honestly. Pride is self-serving, the ugly red cousin of jealousy, and damaging as hell. Being accountable is not an easy thing to do because it requires you to acknowledge you're wrong. To point out your own flaws and be vulnerable.

No one ever wants to do those things. And why would they when it's far easier to hurt someone else's feelings than express their own? Easier to dismiss someone else's opinions while you vehemently defend your own. I'm willing to bet that every argument to ever take place has derived from two things: virtually nothing and someone's failure to take responsibility for their own actions. It's so easy to find fault in what someone else has done. It's especially easy to find fault with someone who isn't even responsible for their own pain. The crazy thing? It doesn't matter whose fault it is when something is broken. What matters is that someone steps up to fix it.

Being back here brought on memories that emanated not only from the very walls themselves but from everything I touched: an old vinyl record, tattered Maya Angelou books, broken sports trophies, old clothes. Even the leafy green plants Granny kept throughout the house whispered their memories. Every morning Granny watered them after putting on a pot of coffee. On Sundays, she watered them while humming to the sound of whatever dustie was playing on the radio. *V103*'s Herb Kent's smooth baritone would float through the house keeping everyone on their toes waiting for him to announce his *Battle of the Bands* segment. It was pure joy. Smelled like a home-cooked meal. Everything was calm and right.

And Granny was at the center of it. She was peaceful, had an electrifying smile, and could light an entire room with just the twinkle in her eyes. She was home. Comfortable, familiar, and always there. A stark contrast from when she wasn't herself, which wasn't often. I can recall two times in my life when I witnessed her truly sad. Both times she sat at the living room table with a cold brew. The only light from the window cast a solemn-looking shadow of Granny on the wall. The faint crackling on her record player let me know she was listening to her vinyls. Powerhouse Dinah Washington blared through the speakers explaining why she didn't hurt anymore. Billie Holiday, Lena Horne, and Etta James were up next. The air felt thick. Almost as if there was none to breathe. We locked eyes. Wordless, but acknowledged a shared understanding.

"I'ma be okay, baby," she'd said the next morning as she watered her plants, "it was just one of those days."

I didn't ask any questions.

Later that evening, our family meeting was an hour late to start, as usual. Cat's incessant banter about her brothers' tardiness was certainly entertaining, especially with Brenda constantly rolling her eyes in response.

"So where Shanice at, Pat?" Brenda queried. My mother sucked her teeth. Brenda smirked. I guess they both have time today.

"Where," Cat abruptly interrupted, "your husband at?"

They both definitely have time today. I sat down on the old worn couch. This was sure to explode. Eli plopped down beside me, unsurprised. "You know your mama don't know how to stop," he laughed.

"I told you he had some business to take care of," Brenda said changing the direction of the elephant figurine beside her. Cat's eyes went black with fury.

She swooped in, nudging Brenda out of the way so she could change it back. "Don't be doing my mama stuff any kind of way."

Brenda stood her ground. Sizing Cat up. She was only a few inches shorter than her. "I don't know why you have a problem. I'm gonna tell my husband about this."

"Tell him," Cat yelled. "He the one should be here anyway."

Heavy footsteps descended the basement stairs. Eli and I exchanged looks in anticipation of who it could be. Whoever it was cleared their throat and spat out what sounded like a lot of phlegm in the laundry room's sink.

"Hey everybody," Chase announced in high spirits. Randy followed behind him and gave a head nod. "I had to take care of some responsibilities."

"This ain't one of them?" Cat asked.

He chuckled at the thought. "Y'all got it."

Terrell rounded the corner, cautiously looking about as if something was missing. Brenda lit up like a kid receiving an ice-cream cone. I guess if it wasn't my uncle I'd think it was cute.

"Y'all know the code to Mama safe?"

"That's why y'all asses here?" My mother was outdone. "Y'all a trip. A got damn trip."

Chase waved her off. "Girl, bye. Y'all doing what y'all supposed to."

She had had enough at that point. It was as if steam protruded from her ears. A yelling match ensued to see who could shut the other one down first. Brenda stood beside her man as if he would tag her in at any moment. Annoyed was not even the word. I sat, massaging my temples. No longer paying attention to what was happening in front of me. Tuning everything out because I was now certain this meeting would never happen.

CHAPTER 9
STATIC NOISE

F aith stood outside the dollhouse, watching her family go about their lives as if no one heard the sounds coming from the upstairs attic. Cat sat in front of the television cackling to the blue corned moon. In the kitchen, Terrell and Randy played dominoes with Spider and friends. Their smiles never faded, and laughs were boisterous as they slammed the pieces down on the table.

"Come on down, woman." Chase yelled from the bottom of the stairs. "Ain't nothing wrong with you."

He sat down, giving attention to whomever he had on the phone. Faith tried to speak but couldn't. Her mouth was zipped shut, her feet planted in cement. With bulging and bewildered eyes, she watched her grandmother pace back and forth at the very top of the house. She wore a white linen house dress stained with blood. She didn't have a heart either. Faith looked right through the hole where her heart should be. She tried to gauge why her grandmother was still alive without her most vital

*organ. She didn't seem to notice. She never said anything, just
paced back and forth like it was the last thing she'd do. Faith
flailed her arms, yelling as loud as she could to get anyone's
attention. No one noticed or heard her. No one went to check
on Granny either.*

From an early age I saw the divide between my mother and
her siblings. I also recognized her need of love and approval
from them. Over the years, she's poured out her heart to me
about her tumultuous relationship with her siblings. Despite
how badly they treat her—and make no mistake, she can dish
it out as well—she can't help but treat them with kindness.
I've seen her curse out a sibling and then defend them in the
same breath. I've seen her drop everything for them when
they needed help, while they only dropped critiques when she
needed succor. I've seen her cook and throw parties for all of
their birthdays, yet when hers comes around, they're gone.
You know what's even more tragic than failing to acknowledge an explosion has occurred? Failing to converse about
its aftereffects. While Cat and her siblings all point fingers
to their parents for the reason why they've never really gotten along, they have never strayed from the shadows of each
other or their parents' home. I've only concluded that parents
do the best they can. Even if it's their worst, unfortunately.

I've also concluded that perception is a bitch. That people
will always find fault in your actions and never hold a mirror
to themselves. Still, you could be blind and see there are deep-
rooted issues between the Moore siblings. I don't know what
happened between them in their youth, but the thin layer of
civility they share is buried below assumptions, jealousy, and
resentment.

Even now, as we sit here awaiting the doctor's prognosis about Granny's second stroke, they cannot operate as a unit. As much as I loved Randy, he never said much. Terrell was the opposite: once he was upset, he never let anyone finish a sentence before he interrupted. Chase was typically unbothered until someone disagreed with his opinion. And my mother? Well, she has a short fuse.

"She need stability." Cat's voice shook lightly.

Chase snorted. "What you know about stability?"

"That ain't cool, bro," Randy said.

Her eyes narrowed. She cast a skeptical eye toward her eldest brother. "What you know about it?"

Their eyes locked in a shared understanding that Chase seemed to never want to admit aloud.

"Y'all should be concerned about getting the combo to Mama safe. We gotta make sure everything in there stay in there."

If my mother had rolled her eyes any harder, I'm sure they'd have popped out of their sockets. "Really? That should be the least of your worries right now. The doctor just told you that this stroke is worse than the first one. Mama need therapy, speech and everything. Let's send her to Rush or Northwestern."

"Don't nobody wanna be driving all the way downtown and stuff," Terrell said, irritated.

"What about Advocate Christ?"

"Uh-uh. Oak Lawn too far, too," Chase said.

"You ungrateful motherfuckers need to be shamed of y'all selves." Aunt Shirley swung her purse's strap over her shoulder, a sure sign that it was time for her to leave. "This ain't about y'all. These people gotta know where my big sister going by Friday, so y'all got three days to get it together. Now, Pat, come with me to the cafeteria so you can help make my coffee, baby."

"Come on, lady."

Pat locked hands with Aunt Shirley, who jerked her head toward her niece and nephews. "Can you believe these doo-doo heads?"

"I'm going," Cat said, following suit. Her brothers mumbled among themselves as they headed toward the elevators. "You want anything, Faith?"

"I'm good, thanks."

I watched them until they disappeared. I couldn't help but wonder how things would be if my family actually got along. Beyond our normal formalities, there wasn't much depth between us. The one exception was Granny. She was the thread that kept us from unraveling. I only wished that we could reciprocate collectively. We're really a beautiful family. We just get in our own way. Are stuck in our ways. And want forgiveness, but won't forgive. Unfortunately, with our family's track record, this isn't surprising. The same dysfunction ensued when Aunt Whitney and Grandaddy Charles were sick. And now it's happening, again, with Granny.

"Excuse me, you're with the Moore family, correct?" A slender nurse stood in front of me. "I'm Mary. One of Ms. Moore's nurses."

"Yes, I'm one of her granddaughters, Faith. Is everything okay?"

"Yes, I'm sorry. Your grandmother is fine." She flushed a bright pink. "I wanted to share some information about a power of attorney with your family. We see families arguing all the time about decisions regarding their loved ones, and it can get pretty bad."

She handed me a few documents. "With a medical power of attorney, someone can act on behalf of Ms. Moore and make healthcare decisions for her if or when she can't do it."

"Thanks, I'll share these with the family."

I wasn't sure if they would be up for it, especially since everyone wanted to be involved. Still, I'd provide Cat and her siblings with the information. Hopefully they'd be able to come to an effective solution. After all, it's all about what's best for Granny. Right?

CHAPTER 10

CRISP DISCOURSE

F aith sat at her grandmother's kitchen table peeling sweet potatoes. Her eyes shift toward Terrell and Granny arguing. He grabs a big pot, fills it with water, then sits on the weathered countertop. Granny, who wears a permanent exasperated look, helps Faith peel the potatoes.

"I already told you I ain't cosigning for no car again. Remember you stopped paying the note last time?"

Terrell throws big leafy greens into the pot, splashing water onto the floor.

"Will you ever grow up, boy?"

"I'ma man, Mama."

"A forty-year-old man that still live with his mama? What kind of man is that?" She shook her head of grayish white hair in disappointment.

"I don't have to be here. And I told you I'm moving out soon."

Faith clears her throat, grabbing the mop to clean up the mess her uncle made. "Terrell, I think she's just asking for you to be more understanding and responsible."

"Nobody was even talking to you. Shouldn't you be heading back to school anyway?"

Frances points the sharp knife toward her son. "You ain't gotta talk to her like that. That's your problem—you don't listen."

"I don't have to deal with this shit," Terrell mutters as he leaves the room.

Frances joins her granddaughter at the kitchen table. "I don't let him bother me, so you best not let him bother you. You hear?"

The sun had begun to set earlier and the temperature dropped to sweater weather. Each day, tension met me when Terrell walked into Granny's room at Sunrise Senior Care, a fifteen-minute car ride from the house. I laid low like morning fog, buried in a book if Granny was asleep or keeping her in good cheer if she was awake. No matter what I did, Terrell looked at me with enough hatred to shrivel my heart. I wanted to give him a few choice words, but instead I bit back my tongue, continuing to commune off my own flesh and blood. I knew Granny wouldn't like it if I disrespected my elder. So I stayed in the background of the arena where he wanted to be lauded—despite other people pulling me center stage. When nurses were present, Aunt Shirley made sure I was paying attention. *You taking notes, baby? I know you like shit like that.* When Cat and her siblings met with the doctor, she included me. *You got any questions?* This was fucked up. I only wanted to be present for my Granny, and I was being vilified for it.

"Comparison is the thief of joy." Dr. Tucker was poised, per usual, and clad in a cute tank and blazer combo via my iPad. I lay in bed with my head tilted back on the old headboard. "We know Terrell isn't happy about your unexpected extended stay. Honestly, Faith, I'm surprised you stayed. I think this is the biggest decision you've made since choosing to attend Gabbie Union's book signing over Janet Jackson's concert."

"Yeah, I was really torn about that."

"So you turned down a case that could fulfill your lifelong dream of becoming partner. How are you feeling?"

"I feel good about being here. Being present for my Granny and siblings. But I'd be remiss if I didn't say I'm not sure when I'll have another career opportunity like that again."

"Having doubts is to be expected in this situation, and it's natural to wonder if you're doing the right thing. How did the partners take it?"

"Although they weren't the happiest about my decision, they understand. But I'll think about all that when I'm headed back."

"And Nicholi?"

"He wasn't surprised. He said he had been waiting on me to realize it."

Dr. Tucker flashed her million-dollar smile. "I've said it a million times before, and I'm saying it again: Nicholi is a good partner. You have to remember that when the little girl inside you needs a hug. Okay," she said putting her pen down. Her face shined brighter than a newly lit candle. "Now let's look at the pros of the situation. Can you name at least two?"

I squeezed my eyes tight, exhaling slow. "Granny is in a place where she can be helped immediately if something happens. The doctors and nurses ensure she's getting the care she needs to get better and come home. And I get to spend more time with her and with family."

"That's great. We know this is a tough time for not only you, but everyone—especially Granny. Remember these pros when Terrell is acting sideways. You can't control how others react to your presence, but you can focus on the positive things."

"That's true."

"Exactly," Dr. Tucker agreed, waving her pen in the air. "Now, that isn't to say the cons can't be fixed. You should try talking to Terrell."

"I'm not sure that's going to help anything."

"Give him a chance. You have to have more faith, Faith."

"Another line that you love, Doc. But he is who he is."

She laughed, sitting back in her chair. "You know I do. But you know what most people don't like?"

"Banana pudding."

"They probably don't. But most people don't like being excluded. They don't like not being heard or misunderstood either."

I threw my hands in the air. "I know that feeling. And I'm not standing in the way or stopping him from doing anything."

"I know. We also know that you aren't going to treat them the way they treat you."

"Well, everyone knows that."

"Listen, you know why you're there, and your presence means a lot to those who want it. As for your uncle, tell him what you told me. If you put some faith in him, you could be pleasantly surprised."

"Or I can be let down."

CHAPTER 11

SIMPLY COMPLEX

The next morning, my phone shivered on the worn dresser for what seemed like the thousandth time. Eight missed phone calls, mostly from Pat, four text messages from Aunt Shirley, and a couple more from Chase. It was 10 a.m. Before I could scan the messages, my room door burst open.

"You ain't got my messages? I know you be up early in the morning cause them motherfuckers in the movies and television don't play baby."

Aunt Shirley was dressed to the nines in a leopard print sweater, gold pants, and black combat boots with a matching fanny pack.

"What's wrong, Shirley?"

"The people asked about some power documents and shit went to hell. I tried to wake your mama but you know her ass sleep like a bear."

My phone rang before I could respond. "Pat, I literally just woke up. I'm on my way."

Another hour of sleep would've been wonderful for this news. Sunrise's cafeteria was painted a cheesy yellow, with even worse orange accents. I poked at a bland-looking salad I didn't want.

"My bad, I forgot. Granny had that second stroke and it slipped my mind. Why would I even want to be her POA?"

"That's what me and Shirley said." Pat sipped her tea. "We were calling you so you could get here this morning. The people asked Terrell if you told us about them papers and his ass said no. Before we knew it, he had asked Granny to pick someone to do it.

"And she chose him?"

"Girl, we was shocked, too. But she said they be arguing too much, so this would make things easier. Honey, you should have seen how he took off to get them papers notarized."

It was funny but sad. The person with a history of mis-handling responsibilities now had the most important one of his life. Pat tapped my hand. I looked up to see Terrell wearing a thousand-watt smile. Brenda followed behind like a love-sick puppy.

"I know y'all heard about what happened," he said, non-chalant. "Everything gonna be fine."

"Yeah," Brenda quipped. "No matter what, we still value y'all's opinion."

Pat looked like a firecracker ready to pop. I nudged her foot below the table. Terrell didn't even seem to notice Brenda.

"Listen," he said. "I'm her son, and I'm what's best." He turned to me. "Shanice told me she saw you open my mama safe. I'm her medical power of attorney now, so you gotta give me the combo."

"Reading is fundamental," I said, pushing my salad aside. "A medical power of attorney only allows you to make decisions regarding her health. And if Granny wants you to have it, she'll give you the combination."

His face remained composed, but his eyes were livid. "Do the right thing, Faith."

He walked away, chin up and chest out, with Brenda's spring in his step.

"You know he ain't playing, right?"

"I know, Pat."

I eased into the flow of traffic. It was a well-known fact that Shirley didn't trust everyone while driving. Her left hand held her right in a tight grip. I tuned the radio quickly, so as not to make her any more nervous than she already was. We were leaving the store, having picked up some more things for Granny. She opened a bag of chips. It was annoying when people ate in my car. Although this was a rental, I felt the same.

"I still can't believe she chose that egg-headed motherfucker to make decisions for her. And that slow-ass fiancée, girlfriend, or whatever she is, can stay the hell away from me. I'm telling you, she's touched, baby."

She ate a couple of chips. As the crunches echoed, I watched crumbs land in her lap. She dusted them off until they hit the floor.

"If I ain't never told you before, I'm proud of you, little lady. You always been strong here," she pointed to her head. "Even when you was little you had control. Now, I ain't gonna lie, you was a little weird. You ain't talk much and you did seem sad, but I just thought it was 'cause you ain't have no hair, baby. They kept you in a onesie and you had a big old bald apple head like Swee Pea. I just knew we was gonna have to buy you some wigs, but the hair came in and ain't stopped since."

"I appreciate that, TT."

We stopped at a red light. I eyed her floor mat anxiously. It took everything in me not to pull over and vacuum it. Shirley gripped my shoulder. We locked eyes. "You always been quiet and kind. Don't let people take your kindness for a weakness."

Our phones pinged at the same time. Shirley looked at her phone. "This motherfucker is crazy."

I checked my phone. Terrell had texted the family group chat.

Today Mama being moved to ManorCare in Frankfort. I just left. Someone needs to go be with her.

A second later my phone pinged with a response from Pat. *You have to be freaking kidding! That's at least thirty minutes from the house. I thought they ain't wanna travel?*

I replied quickly. *I'm on my way with Shirley.*

Making a U-turn at the light, I headed for the expressway. It was a quiet ride. Or rather, it was for me, as I mostly listened to Shirley rant about the situation.

"It's just a shame the way he going about this. My big sister need stability. She need therapy if she gonna get better." She pounded her fist on one knee like Granny did. "She ain't gonna get better if that shit ain't happening. I told his milk dud head ass that."

Shirley was a CNA for thirty-five years, so I knew she was sure of what she spoke about. It was a rare occasion to see her upset, as she was generally sweet with a bit of spice.

"I don't want to get involved, Faith." She damn near threw her bag of chips in the air. "That's my big sister," she muttered. "But those her kids, and that's what she want."

"You know I completely agree, Shirley. We'll figure it out."

She fingered her wedding ring. I was amazed that she still wore it after all these years. When I finally asked her about it a few years ago, she said it brought her comfort. Her husband died when I was young. I remember Aunt Shirley and Travis lived in Block 3 in the Gardens, and Aunt Whitney stayed over in Block 7. My cousins and I would run back and forth between the rows, stopping at the corner store for ice cups and candy. Shirley and Travis's apartment smelled like incense and coffee. They drank coffee five to six times each day. When I stayed over, I was allowed to bring them their morning cups from the kitchen to the living room table. Travis always added some cream; Shirley preferred hers black.

"I like my coffee how I like my man," she explained one day.

We had a hopscotch board permanently chalked out front where we played daily. Shirley would sit in her wicker chair while Travis prepared dinner. They always had a smile on their faces. There was always laughter and jokes. I loved being there because I felt at ease, safe. I miss my uncle.

"You know our mama had had a stroke and ended up in the hospital, too," Shirley recalled. "Your Granny, me and Ray went back and forth constantly with Marie about all her affairs."

Aunt Marie was the eldest, and had passed away five years ago. Uncle Ray, their youngest sibling, now lived in Arizona. "Mama had told me to handle her things because I was always helping her. She was living in the city on 44th and King, and everybody else was out in the suburbs."

Shirley stared out the window. "Marie wouldn't have it because I was the youngest. I was scared of her," she chuckled. "Marie wasn't nothing to play with. But I stood my ground and did what Mama told me to. Oh, she cursed me out every time she saw me. Told everybody I was stealing all Mama jewelry, clothes and shit." She turned to me suddenly. "Can you believe that? My own sister lying on me."

I thought it was interesting that history had a habit of repeating itself. No one had ever really shared the details of what happened when Grandma Dot passed. I only knew that shit got real and everyone had their own version of a story to share like petty reality TV celebrities. All I could do was listen and hope that the past didn't come back to haunt us.

CHAPTER 12
DEJA VU

P at tapped her foot impatiently. She glanced at Granny and let out a heavy sigh. For the past two weeks, Granny had been in and out of consciousness, uttering incoherently, and drooled at the mouth more often than not. It was a sad sight to see for everyone who came to visit her, which wasn't many at this point.

"This ain't right, Faith," her voice cracked. "She stay drowsy and can't even have therapy."

"Cat said she talked to her brother and he told her he would talk to the doctor, but that was last week."

"Something gotta change, man, for real."

A throat cleared from the doorway. A small woman, with an even smaller voice, knocked on the door. "I'm sorry for interrupting, but I'm looking for Terrell. Is he here?"

Pat stood at attention. "No, not since this morning."

"I'm Patricia Wentworth, the financial officer here at ManorCare." She eyed her watch anxiously. "Terrell was supposed to meet me an hour ago to discuss Ms. Moore's payments. I've called a few times but haven't been able to reach him."

Pat raised her eyebrows at me. I was just as jarred as she was, so I shrugged in return. "I'm sorry about that. Is there anything we can do to help? The family wasn't aware of any payments that needed to be made."

"When Ms. Moore was transferred here, I informed Terrell that her insurance would only fully cover her stay for eighteen days, which ends this coming Tuesday. I know it's a few days away, but we just want to ensure it's taken care of." Both Pat's and my jaws could've hit the floor. "We're going into a new month and her co-pay to stay is forty dollars daily. However, we prefer six hundred dollars is paid up front for half the month, and then we'll discuss payment options from there."

"Ms. Wentworth, again, we had no idea," I said. "But thanks for letting us know. We will get this resolved as soon as possible. Also, is it possible to have her dosage lowered? How can she have therapy if she can't function?"

"I'm sorry, she isn't having therapy. We informed Terrell that he had ten days from the day she was admitted here to opt her in, and he never did." She paused, examining her watch again. "Would either of you be interested in being put on file as a second point of contact for Ms. Moore? We need to be able to reach someone if anything should happen."

Back at the house, I massaged my temples counterclockwise. For the last twenty minutes, all Cat had done was go back and forth with Brenda. Shit hit the fan after Pat told our mother what happened with Ms. Wentworth this morning. She called

Shirley, who called and left a bunch of not-so-polite voice-mails on Terrell's phone, as well as a family meeting to discuss what could be done. It hadn't gone as planned.

"My husband asked me to come on his behalf," Brenda said, flipping her long weave out of her face. "Like I said, he thinks we should use Ma's card to pay for her to stay."

Cat pointed a finger at her. "We already told you the family agreed months ago to not use her cards for anything. And that was your husband idea."

Brenda sneered, "That don't matter now. Ain't nobody got the money to put up for this. Unless Faith want to pay again?"

"You motherfuckers ain't even gave her the money back from the last time," Shirley snapped. "Y'all her kids, right? Split the damn bill and figure out the rest of the month. And you tell your Ninja Turtle–looking ass husband he should be ashamed of himself for not signing her up for therapy. Ole ugly self."

Brenda looked as if she was going to respond. "When I say something to you, don't say shit back," Shirley continued. "I ain't the one."

The sly look on Brenda's face welcomed any remarks that came her way. "Actually, my husband did want me to ask one thing. He wants to know when Faith's gonna give him the code to the safe." Her sly grin grew wide.

"Tell yo' damn husband he shoulda been here to ask about it," Cat quipped. She sat up so quick in her seat I thought she was going to charge right up to Brenda.

I've always been amazed at how quickly my mother was able to get angry. Her personality was like a firecracker, which at times could be a good thing. She could be fun to be around, but she could also get dangerous hot and hurt anyone in her way. Right now she was the latter.

"He should be more concerned with his mama and being there for her," she added, fuming. "Ain't shit in that safe he need."

My siblings and I exchanged humorous looks. We knew, just like the rest of the family, that once one of Granny's kids got going they seemed to never want to stop.

Brenda sucked her teeth. "He just wanna see if her life insurance policy in there so he can see who the beneficiary is." She looked as if she had said too much.

"His bowling ball faced ass concerned about the wrong shit," Shirley said.

"She's right," I agreed.

Brenda sucked her teeth even louder: "That may be true, little girl, but that's still his mama and you're her granddaughter."

I heard Pat gasp in shock. I laughed. Hard. "This is true. But don't mitigate what I bring to the table just because of that. After all, I'm the granddaughter who knows the code, and he's the son who doesn't."

"Goofy bitch," Cat spewed with much venom.

"All right, Cat, calm down," Shirley interjected. "You know the girl gotta try to be tough. Frances is the priority here, so let's stay focused on her cause she what's important."

"It's all good, Auntie," she said, standing to go. "And I'm out on that note."

CHAPTER 13

BROKENHEARTED

"I don't ever want to feel like that again."

Granny clutched Pat's and my hands as if she'd get lost if she let go. Her doctor had finally lowered the dosage of her opioids a couple of days ago, and most of us had been waiting for her to come out of her daze. She finally had a breakthrough at dinner but refused to eat the slop in front of her.

"Where is Shanice? Randy and everybody else?" she asked, perplexed. "Come here, Eli, give me a hug, baby."

"Randy and Chase was here this morning, but they left 'cause you usually knocked out," Shirley explained.

"Cat and Patience went to the cafeteria to get some food." Eli gave Granny a big kiss on the forehead.

"Shanice and Took moved out a few weeks ago," I said. "We're keeping her updated with what's happening. She says she'll try to visit soon."

Granny dropped her head. It was the saddest thing I'd ever seen. Lips quivering. Eyes washed over like waves preparing to crash against the shore. Her right hand gripped the left like a child that didn't want to let their mother go. "I guess since I can't help nobody no more, nobody need me or love me."

My heart shrank. Shattered into a million pieces. I struggled to swallow the lump in my throat. Struggled to keep the tears from spilling out. Struggled to find the right words to say, but they evaded me like a cat near water. I wished I could wrap her up in my arms and let my heart speak the words my mouth couldn't find. I wished that whenever she felt this way she could be encompassed by and reassured with the abundant love of those who are in her corner one thousand percent. I wished that the presence of those actually around could make up for those who should be here. Unfortunately, that isn't the case. The heart always wants what it wants. And that's okay.

I know Granny appreciated the presence of those she saw regularly. However, it didn't take a rocket scientist to know that the presence of all her kids and Shanice—who she may as well have given birth to since she raised—were equally if not more important. And I totally understood why. I don't believe it's because she loves them more than the rest of us. I believe it's because she's always gone above and beyond for them, and now she expects them to reciprocate. She isn't wrong. Honestly, we should all be moving mountains right now for her. But what can you do about another person's actions? Nothing. All you can do is your part.

"Don't let these fools make you feel bad, Frances," Shirley said, caressing her sister's hair. "You know Shanice ass gonna pop up soon 'cause her and Took gonna get into it like always. And them weirdo boys of yours will be here. I'ma text they ass now. Eli, come text your crazy uncles for me, baby."

Granny picked at the tray of food in front of her. The doctor said she could only eat puréed food. She wasn't a fan of it. I didn't blame her. Everything on her plate looked like applesauce. She ate a few spoonfuls of her pudding. It seemed to calm her.

"Eli, how you doing in school?" she asked. "You getting yourself together?"

"Yeah," he said as Shirley looked at him, amazed at his texting speed. "I'm passing all my classes."

"Good, baby. You got two years left then you can graduate and make something of yourself and life."

"Right," Shirley snorted, "unlike these men in the family."

"He ain't gonna be nothing like these men in the family," Cat said, striding into the room.

"Y'all be nice," Granny said, eating another spoonful. "It's hard being a Black man in this world."

"And it's even harder being a Black woman," Shirley scoffed. "They treat us worse and then they think they can come home and throw shit at us too."

"This is true, but you know we built for this. We ain't never had a choice. And I ain't saying that make it any better 'cause the load is heavy, honey." Granny paused to sip from the cup of water her sister held to her lips. "That's why you gotta take care of here and here," she told Eli, pointing to her heart and mind. "Us too, but at least we know how to deal with multiple things at one time."

"That is true," Shirley echoed her big sister. "That's why you take care of your heart and mind, and then you find a woman that done did the same thing. Chile, you do that and ain't nobody gonna be able to stop y'all."

CHAPTER 14

STANDING FIRM

C at picked at a napkin while I yawned over the hot cup of tea before me. We hadn't had a proper night's sleep since Granny had been moved to a new home, The Villa. My mama, Pat, Shirley, and I were alternating shifts. I stayed overnight most evenings, as I didn't have any children, work, or a husband, in-state, to care for. Of course, her sons popped in when they could. Chase specifically let his stance be known.

"That ain't my responsibility," he'd said when asked when he would be able to take a shift.

"Y'all look horrible." Terrell took a seat at the cafeteria's table. He, of course, looked well rested and glowing.

Cat glared at him so hard I thought he would keel over. "You know we been staying nights to keep Mama company. She say the nurses bothering her."

He shrugged half-heartedly. "You know she dramatic."

"Whatever she is, she our mother," she said, mocking him. "And she won't get better if you keep moving her around. This the second home she been moved to. She ain't had consistent therapy or nothing."

Even with her cold eyes boring through him, Terrell's smirk was colder. "She got stability."

"She deserves better," I interjected. "If we can all come together, I think we would really encourage Granny and help her recovery."

Drops of tea splashed out of the cups as his clenched fists banged on the table, staining the white tablecloth. "This ain't no courtroom and your word ain't law. Y'all need to let me do what I need to."

Cat's voice didn't waver. "Well, do it. This about Frances. If you gonna be in control, do what you supposed to do."

"Like you?" He wiped his jacket's lapel, though there was nothing there. "Do you do what you supposed to do?"

Cat was stoic. Terrell was unbothered. They glared at each other for what seemed like forever.

"Have you ever done what you supposed to?" she asked him.

I poured more ginger into my tea. The pungent, peppery scent lingered in the air, reminding me of the day I had ginger and tea for the first time. I was ten years old on that warm, sunny day. Aunt Whitney sat with me at Granny's kitchen table. She was, and still is, the funniest person I've ever known. Aunt Whitney had a gorgeous smile and the personality to match. Her boisterous laugh was endearing, but it didn't fit her slender frame.

We waited for the tea to steep while she taught me how to play solitaire. She loved playing the game and assured me that if I learned how to play, I'd love it as well. I didn't doubt her, as her words were golden in my life. Not only because she was the best aunt in the world, but also because she introduced me to Janet Jackson's *The Velvet Rope*. I instantly loved Janet just as much as she did.

"You know I taught her some of those dance moves," she said mimicking the moves from *If*.

"You did?" My eyes widened and mind was blown.

"Sure did." Her rosy face shined bright. "We met at a club one night when we were teenagers. We were both in dance crews. She saw me dancing with one of my teammates and took our whole routine. No one can move a man's head like that but me, honey."

The teapot whistled like a train right after I pulled the King of Diamonds.

"You can start a new pile with that," she called over her shoulder. I watched her move with ease as she grabbed the honey, sugar, and ginger from the corner cabinet. "Ginger is good for you," she noted, pouring tea into our cups. It smelled warm and innocent until she added all the ingredients, especially the ginger. It gave it some spice and tickled my nose as she put two spoonfuls in each of our cups. "It can help get rid of inflammation in our bodies."

I didn't know what inflammation was, but I didn't want to interrupt her. So I made a mental note to look it up in my dictionary later that night. Mama came into the room disheveled. Hair was all over her head, eyes red and puffy. Aunt Whitney spoke gently.

"Have some tea with us, Cat." She pulled the adjacent chair to hers out from underneath the table. "You can teach Faith how to play solitaire, too."

Mama grumpily rummaged through the fridge. "My stomach upset." She cleared her throat and spit thick phlegm into the trash can. "I just need to eat something and go back to bed."

Aunt Whitney held out her cup. "Ginger is a great remedy for that. Take a seat and have some."

Cat took the cup and drank. Just as she was about to sit, Terrell came into the kitchen. The two stiffened at the sight of each other.

He wrinkled his nose. "If you were at home more, Whitney and Francis wouldn't have to look after your kids."

Cat's lips curled. "You always got something to say. Why don't you just leave me alone? Worry about your kids that you don't raise or support, deadbeat."

Terrell's eyes flashed red. "You can take your ass on and get out," he yelled.

"This Frances house. You don't run shit here."

Aunt Whitney tried to calm them both down. "Both of y'all need to shut up because neither of you are parent of the year. So take that mess somewhere else."

I wondered how Aunt Whitney would handle this situation now. Here her siblings were twenty-something years later, still arguing over what the other did or did not do. Missing the point as always. I sipped my tea, watching them go back and forth. I guess the lesson learned here was that time waited on no one. That growth was a daily choice we all had to make. And remembering that it takes two fools to argue.

"Are you sure you responsible?" Cat asked, arching a single eyebrow. "You don't even answer her doctor calls. They can't even get in touch with you when something happens. That's why Faith and me are now emergency contacts."

He looked from mama to me in disbelief. "Y'all just wanna be in control and make all the decisions."

"It's not about that for me. Granny is y'all's mother, so that's y'all's responsibility. But I will help out where she asks me. Being an emergency contact isn't overstepping any boundaries. We should be able to work together, Terrell. We all want what's best for Granny, right?"

He leaned in close to me. His hot breath grazing my nostrils. "I am what's best."

I heard Shirley's voice echoing in my head, *Don't let people take your kindness for a weakness.*

"I don't think you are. This is bigger than the both of us. This is Granny's livelihood here."

He chuckled and wagged his fat fingers in my face. "Oh, so because you got some degrees and you a lawyer you know best?"

I glanced at my mama. Her hard gaze never left her brother's direction, but I recognized the head nod she gave me to stand my ground.

"No. I don't know best. I just know I can help. And my education helps as well. I'm not walking away from my granny because of you."

I saw the flash of excitement in his eyes. Saw him savor, then swallow the taste of satisfaction from this moment.

"You'll walk away one way or another."

CHAPTER 15
STILL BLUE

I didn't always find comfort in silence and being numb. Reading and music are the only two ways I've truly felt at ease. Whether it's a song, book, or note scribbled on a pad, words are chosen carefully. Even if they're trash. I love the infinite ways you can assemble them. Thoroughly enjoy how you can say one thing in a million ways. I feel words. It's like we share a bond that no one else cares to understand. I always wanted to have meaning in my life. Reading and music provided that. MC Lyte and Queen Latifah inspired me to put pen to paper. Langston Hughes confirmed that I was a poet. Maya Angelou affirmed that I had a story to tell. Toni Morrison shined a light on loving me.

I was about ten years old the day I decided I wouldn't let my family affect me anymore. For the life of me, I can't remember why we gathered. It wasn't a holiday but I remember there was an abundance of food: oven-baked macaroni and cheese, red beans and rice, corn bread, fried chicken, potato salad, and caramel cake. Good music filled the house, including Bloodstone, the Temptations, Barry White, and the Whispers. At that time, my grandparents lived in Markham, a Cook County city known for its pine trees. It was the first home I remember. The suburban city was everything it sounded like: single-family homes with white picket fences, lush green lawns, and friendly neighbors. That's exactly how it was. Neighbors actually knew each other. Children rode their bikes freely throughout the nearly six-mile city. My cousins and I raced up and down the blocks with abandon.

I'll never forget the green house with white shutters and a white screen door to match. A huge pine tree sat right in the middle of the lawn; a smaller version sat adjacent to the gravel driveway and served as a hiding place for when we were in trouble. Cookie, my grandparents' German Shepard, stayed tied up on the side of the garage. She was an evil dog. One day I was walking up the driveway after school and she broke loose from her chain just as I reached the side door's steps. Cookie chased me around Granddaddy Charles's black Astro van. Fortunately, he grabbed me right before she tore into my legs. The side door led to the back room. It was like any common gathering area in a home: a couple of recliners and green couches. A huge entertainment system not only held a big screen TV but also hundreds of CDs and records. The brick fireplace provided comfort during winter. Granny's colorful jukebox sat in the far corner of the room. My cousins and I would always beg her to play Johnnie Taylor's "Last Two Dollars" and Tyrone Davis's "Mom's Apple Pie." At the time, it was the warmest room I'd ever been in. And not because of the fireplace. House music compelled my cousins to have dance battles. During the summer, we'd sprawl on the floor with markers and crayons making fliers for our family cleaning business. On other days we'd write songs together, harmonizing the melodies until we finally got them right. Our biggest hit was "Baby, Baby," an ode to that special person we loved. During our sleepovers, we'd make thick pallets on the floor and watch *Blankman, Good Burger,* and *Crooklyn.*

I was very observant. And on this particular day, I realized that it's not just rooms that held energies; people did too. I sat on the edge of the fireplace—I can still hear the soft cracklings—looking about the room and then through the open double doors that led to the kitchen. Randy sat in a recliner sneaking Pat—clad in a pink onesie with a small Afro—sips of ginger beer. To my right, Whitney danced with Mama and Chase, while Shanice played Connect Four with Terrell. In the kitchen, Granny and Granddaddy Charles moved in harmony preparing dinner. It went on like that for some time. Observing. Sneaking. Dancing. Playing. Prepping. Gradually, the adults drank more liquor. Words were said. Eyes were cut. Postures stiffened. Egos surfaced. Prides swelled. The room was blazing hot. I cried. Then shudder-inducing cold engulfed the room. And swallowed me.

"Stop it," I yelled.

"Be quiet," someone barked.

So I did. With tears streaming down my face. With my heart pounding. With a formidable lump in my throat. I was quiet. And remained that way whenever something happened as the years tumbled on. I picked up a pen to release the words I couldn't utter, until the tears no longer spilled over when something happened. The lump in my throat became a pebble. My words were only heard on the pages I wrote on. The overwhelming emotion I once felt was now fleeting, like pollen on the wind. Despite these coping mechanisms, it wasn't until I started therapy that I realized I suffered from post-traumatic stress disorder. Sounds crazy, right?

But it made sense. Although I hadn't gone off to fight in a war, the warfare that took place within my family had the same emotional and psychological implications. There was a constant battle. Damn near every day. For years.

Dealing with people can be very exhausting. It's even worse when it's family. Many of us are so self-centered that we aren't willing to meet another's needs if they don't meet ours first. And even then, there's a chance we still won't adhere. Respect is such a skewed concept. Everyone wants it but aren't willing to give it. Respect takes work. And genuine respect takes time to cultivate. You can't treat someone less-than and expect them to think and treat you like you're sensational. It all circles back to a lack of accountability, of which my family are the poster children. Regardless, fifteen years later, I'm still deemed a smartass. Fifteen years later, I still ponder why some families require your silence. Fifteen years later, my checkbook is more valuable than my presence.

CHAPTER 16
CATCHING PREY

Granny slept peacefully. It was 8:30 p.m. Typically she was awake when I came at this time. Everyone was usually gone as well, and tonight was no different. My feet tapped to the sound of the music. Her iPod played "I Can't Get over You" by the Dramatics. My ears perked up as heavy, quick footsteps neared the room. Terrell slithered in. He flicked something, which was likely nothing, off the arm of his sports jacket. I didn't have to look at his shoes to see they were shining like new money.

"Them insurance papers ain't in Mama safe. She told me you got them. You need to give them to me."

The small table lamp cast a glimpse of his harrowing face. "You think this is some kind of game? That I'm a joke or something?" he continued, his eyes locked on me.

"This isn't about you."

He took four cool steps toward me. "Look, I get it. Mama always been there for you. She been there for all of us."

Terrell flailed his arms about the room as if the whole family was here. He didn't have to come any closer for me to see, or smell, that he had been drinking. I could tell by the way he swayed. Heard the slight slur in his tone.

"I know I ain't made the best decisions. But you gotta give me a chance to lead. This my mama." He pointed at Granny, who was still sleeping. "You're a grandchild and you ain't got no right here. Let me take care of her. That's why I'm here. All of her burdens should be on me and my siblings."

I gripped the sides of the chair. He was right. I didn't have to go through all of this, especially this bullshit with him. I could give up the papers and let her children handle everything. That would be the easier route. However, if they fucked up I'd feel like shit when I knew what it was from the beginning.

"You ain't gonna give them to me, huh?"

It took less than a second, but I saw it. The moment he transformed into another person. His eyes were feverish. Rage seeped through his pores. Teeth bared. A wicked sensation tingled down my spine. He snatched me out of the chair like a cat catching its dinner. Gripping the collars of my jacket. Pulled my face close enough to smell the Hennessy raging on his tongue. I caught a glimpse of Granny out of my peripheral. Mouth open and wide-eyed.

"Let her go, Terrell," she yelled, hoarse. The tears fell from her eyes like rain from a weeping willow. "Y'all need to just stop."

We tussled out of the room into the hallway. Knocking pictures off the walls. I refused to hit him because I didn't want him to swing. Let's be honest. He was at least a hundred pounds heavier and a foot taller than me. I wouldn't be able to handle that hit. I tried to kick him in the balls, but, surprisingly, he was quick on his feet. The nurses yelled for him to stop. I could only imagine what we looked like: a bear playing with a rag doll.

"She's my mama," he hissed. His hand coiled around my neck like a snake, the other checked my pockets until he found my wallet. "Until you give me them papers, you ain't gonna have this."

My teeth broke through the skin on his wrists. I tasted blood. Metallic. Warm. Purely fucking disgusting. He yelled in anguish, throwing me against the wall. Air rushed back into my lungs like sinners to church on First Sunday.

"Fucking bitch." I ducked just in time. His hand went right through the wall. I stared at the gaping hole where my head would have been. Terrell grasped his wrist, heading toward the lobby.

"Give me my wallet," I gasped. The nurses followed me, advising to let him go. They were more livid than me. As we neared the entrance, two policemen came through the doors. Brenda followed suit right behind them.

"He attacked this woman and took her wallet," one of the elder nurses explained.

The blond, blue-eyed cop grabbed Terrell and put his arms behind his back. He took my wallet out of his hands and gave it to his partner.

"Is this yours ma'am?" the officer asked, handing it to me. He wore wire-rimmed eyeglasses. "Do you want to press charges?"

My head hung. Then looked up to see Terrell's dead eyes. "It is. And I do."

Officer Blue Eyes cuffed Terrell and mirandized him. Brenda lost her shit.

"This is bullshit," she shouted. "My husband ain't do nothing wrong. He just trying to get his mama insurance papers from her. She won't give them to him."

Officer Eyeglasses looked from me to Terrell. "Is this true?"

"Yes, officer," Terrell said with pleading eyes. He and his wife deserved an Oscar for this performance. "She the granddaughter and I'm the son. She been spending her money, too."

"That's bullshit and you know it," I spat. "Granny asked me to hold on to them papers."

Officer Eyeglasses scrutinized me. "If you've been spending this woman's money, that's a felony. You could be in big trouble if you're lying."

I couldn't believe this bullshit was happening. People in the world could not be this simple. "I haven't spent any of her money, so I'm not worried, Officer."

"Are you being a smartass?" Officer Eyeglasses took a few steps toward me. "Because that won't help this situation."

"I'm a lawyer." If I could curse out these officers I would. But I had to remain calm for my own sake. "I know the law and wouldn't break it."

Officer Eyeglasses backed down a bit. "Well, be that as it may, as a grandchild you have no right to be in possession of your grandmother's insurance papers when she has living offspring." He gestured to his partner. "Uncuff him."

I ran my hands through my hair. "So that's it? Even though he attacked me, stole my wallet, and tried to leave the premises you aren't going to arrest him?"

Officer Eyeglasses half-shrugged. "We see these family disputes all the time. Stuff happens. Now let's go see who this lady would like to have her papers."

Brenda tended to Terrell's wrist. My eyes darted from her lackluster face to her cheap weave. The both of them made my damn skin itch.

The nurse was soothing Granny when we entered her room. Her wet eyes were red and puffy. When she saw me she outstretched her arms. I folded into them, kissing her hands. "I'm okay, lady. Just calm down, all right."

"Terrell, you should be ashamed of yourself," she said. "That wasn't right." He tried to protest, but she didn't want to hear it. "That wasn't right."

He stood pouting in the middle of the room like a spoiled brat.

"Ms. Moore's blood pressure is really high," the nurse said. "She needs to calm down and rest. We're asking everyone to leave for the night."

Officer Blue Eyes cleared his throat. "We understand that, ma'am. We just need her to decide who she would like to have her insurance papers."

"Keep them in the office here for me," she said, weary. "This is just too much. It don't make no sense for all this to be happening."

I caressed her hands. "I'll bring them tomorrow."

Terrell was irate. "See, she ain't doing what she say. You need to give them to her now."

Officer Eyeglasses approached him with his hand on his taser. "I need you to calm down, sir. She said she'll bring them tomorrow."

The nurse waved us all out. "All right, it's time to go."

I kissed Granny's hands once more. "I'm sorry about tonight, lady."

She squeezed mine tight. "It ain't your fault, baby."

Officer Blue Eyes walked me to my car and left. I sat behind the wheel in frustration and let out a wail. Pounding the steering wheel, wishing it was Terrell and his wife's dog-like face. I felt like I should be crying. Not one tear fell.

I'd never felt so weak before in my life. Never felt so shitty. Never felt so violated. This is why family took advantage of me. If you didn't degrade or swear them to hell, they thought they could walk all over you. For me, it has never just been about treating family with respect for the hell of it.

I never did it out of fear. Never did it to keep the peace. Never did it just because my Granny told me to, although pleasing her is high on my list. It's always been about not spewing words that I knew I wouldn't regret. Words that I knew wouldn't make me feel bad but them. Words that I knew I wouldn't apologize for. I started the engine.

CHAPTER 17
SWEET CHAOS

"Are you okay?" Shirley rode with me to the senior home this morning. There was a crisp chill in the air. Brown, red, and orange leaves fell from the trees. They crinkled underneath the weight of my Michael Kors boots.

"I'll be fine. But her papers will be put in the home's safe while she remains in their care. That's what she wants."

We heard the horrible rumblings of the thing that could only be Terrell's car pulling into the parking lot. Birdie's grip tightened on her purse's strap as he and Brenda got out of the car. The look on his pathetic face said that he was unmoved, while his wife just looked stank as they approached.

Shirley brandished a pistol from her bag. "You got some motherfucking nerve putting your hands on her. Next time, pick on somebody your own size."

Terrell stopped in his tracks. "Worry about your own business."

Brenda stood next to her husband, smacking her lips. I was sure I could remove ninety percent of her beauty with a wet Kleenex. "Someone had to put her in her place."

"When you have something to say, tell your man."

Brenda took a step forward. "Listen—"

Shirley shot a bullet into the air. "Didn't I tell your biscuit body ass when I say something don't say nothing back to me?"

Brenda was mum.

"Don't say shit else to me, Faith, or anyone else in this family," Shirley shouted. She reloaded her gun and pointed it at Terrell. "As for you, if you touch her again you gonna have to deal with me."

The smug look crept back onto his face. "Promise?"

"You're not talking me out of this, Faith. I'm on the next flight out. Besides, it's been too long since I've held you. I'll see you tonight."

Nicholi took a leave of absence from work and declared he wouldn't leave my side until I came home. There was nothing I could say to keep that man away now.

"I'll see you soon. Love you, babe."

I turned off the radio and plopped down on the bed. Squeezed my eyes shut, then inhaled deep. My ears perked up hearing music playing in the next room. Mama's room. I looked at my watch. She wasn't supposed to be back from her meeting for another hour. I stood in the small hallway space in between our rooms and opened her door.

She paced back and forth, mumbling. Cigarette in one hand, a cup of only what could be liquor in the other. She was drunk. "Cat, what's going on?"

"Hey, Faith," she slurred. She smiled wide. "I'm just playing solitaire." She motioned to the cards on the bed. My eyes followed her hand and fell on a pipe. She put her cup down and tried to hide it, but it was too late.

"I ain't used it, I promise." Her shrill laugh took me back to my youth when I'd come home and find her high. I looked at her face closely. Her eyes were glassy.

My walls went up. "Are you all right?"

She sighed heavy. Took a long puff of her cigarette, then sipped from her cup. "Yes, but no. It's what I was given. Every day I go out and see these people." Tears fell from her eyes silently like a monk. "I try to do right by my mama."

I leaned on the nearby dresser. What had already been an emotionally draining twenty-four hours was sure to be even longer now.

"And I know I was a bad mother to y'all. I did the best I could do," she said with furrowed brow. "Well, I know I ain't really do my best. But I thought I was doing better than my parents. I hope y'all can forgive me."

"All of that was so long ago, Cat. If we've let it go, you have to as well."

Aretha Franklin's "Share Your Love with Me" played on her phone. "That's my jam." She snapped her fingers and started to step by herself. Seeing Cat dance was one of the things I loved most. She was confident. Radiant. Smooth like butter.

"It's an evil wind . . . that blows no good, yeah," she sang along with Aretha. "It's a sad heart . . . that won't love like I know it should. . . . Honestly, on everything, y'all have had a better life than I have had. I never had a chance. Never had an option. Ain't even go to school because I was either sick or helping my parents out."

She pulled a bottle of tequila out of her purse and poured another cup. "Didn't I always tell y'all, y'all better not ever go against each other?" I nodded, giving her a weak smile. "You and your siblings. Y'all all each other got. Y'all won't never have to fight each other. I had to fight my siblings because my parents made a difference with their children. I ain't make none with mine."

She took an uneven step, her shoulders drooping. "My father, your Granddaddy Charles, I ain't even know what I had until he died," she choked out the words.

"Out of everything I have done for my family, I don't mean shit to them." She started playing solitaire. Wiping at her bloodshot eyes. "I ain't worth shit to nobody."

"You have to realize your own worth, Cat. It doesn't matter who doesn't see your value. You have to see it. That's where it starts."

She looked at me, curious. "Where that come from?"

"Within. You have to love yourself regardless of who doesn't."

Her pained face broke me. "What is love?" she asked. "What does love feel like?" She downed the rest of her cup in one gulp. "You know what? I don't even give a fuck."

CHAPTER 18

RELAX. RELATE. RELEASE.

Nicholi massaged my tense shoulders. His warm hands worked magic as Anita Baker's "Whatever It Takes" sauntered through the room. My soul received the songstress' mature sounds as if they were rain on dry ground. We stood in front of our suite's window overlooking Chicago's mesmerizing skyline. Dusk bid adieu to the day and stretched across the sky like the perfect hues of a tequila sunrise. I was besotted. Not by alcohol, but rather, the aroma of my husband's aura. His enchanted hands reached my waist, wrapping themselves tight around my frame.

"What do you need tonight?" His fingertips grazed my arms the way two lovers' hands touch in passing.

A warmth rushed through me that I had been longing for. "Unbridled passion."

Trapped between the window and a hard place, my robe fell to the floor like a feather in the breeze. I pursued my assailant just as viscously, but to no purpose; he was in control. Soft but wet lips traveled the length of my collarbone and bulbous breasts, and finally suckled my nipples. Pinning him on his back, I wanted to take part in the sucking and licking, too. My husband, however, detoured me from reaching my destination. He held me by the shoulders, kissing my forehead.

"Are you okay?"

"Yes."

"If you weren't would you tell me?"

"No."

"Haven't I proven myself to you? After all these years?"

"Of course."

"Then act like it. Talk to me, Faith."

"I don't feel like talking. What? You wanna hear me say that I'm hurt? That I feel violated? That I'm angry as fuck?"

"If that's how you feel. Look at me." He cupped my chin. "I know you're used to being strong because you've always had to. I also know that some days the load is too much to bear. That's why I'm here."

"You asked me what I needed tonight," I said with my eyes squeezed shut. "I need you." It was true. I didn't want to talk about the horrendous pain I felt. I wanted to feel good. The words surged through my body and fell from my lips again, "Baby, I need you."

Nicholi's silence made me squeeze my eyes even tighter.

"Get on the bed. Lie on your stomach." He rummaged through his bags until he found what he was looking for. "You remember the first time I gave you a massage?"

"Yeah, it was a setup. Who rolls around with massage oil on the ready like that? You know what you were doing."

The oil warmed as his magnificent hands maneuvered up and down my spine.

"You're right. I knew these hands were magic. I told you these hands where magic. Told you these hands were gonna remove brain tumors and save lives. I also told you that these hands would save you. And you said what, Mrs. Shields?"

"I don't need to be saved. But if you insist, I'm gonna save you, too."

"Right. We have saved each other, baby." Moans rose from the depth of my belly as he applied pressure to my lower back. "And we will continue to do so. But you have to let me in. We are partners. I work to give you the best of me. I need you to receive and reciprocate."

Nicholi squeezed more oil into his hands as the Whispers' "Say Yes" prodded me in the right direction.

"I hear you, babe."

"Good. Now I want you to feel me." His thick tongue circled figure eights across my ass. My reflex caused me to stretch and arch. He caught my hike and then proceeded to tickle my cervix. "Now, tell me how much you need me."

CHAPTER 19

BAG LADY

E veryone is different when it comes to trauma. Our experiences, reactions, and resilience are unique; however, we all carry it the same: heavy and burdened. And we all store it the same, too. Trauma is stored in the limbic region, one of the oldest parts of the brain. Back when we were cave people and encountered a threat, our amygdala sent signals to the rest of the body. This signal triggers an automatic process called fight or flight. If the threat is close, there's no time for the amygdala to communicate with the prefrontal cortex, which is responsible for logic, reason, and higher cognitive functioning. So when we experience a traumatic event and cannot escape the threat, the experience remains in the nonverbal parts of the limbic region.

"Many of us carry baggage, Faith. Let's think of it as your favorite backpack," Dr. Tucker said, clever as always. "You fill it with what you want to carry. What's some of your favorite things you like to carry with you? Only consider essential items."

"I always carry a book, some pens and paper, body oil, my iPad, mascara, lip gloss, baby wipes, and earbuds."

"Good!" Dr. Tucker was excited. "I bet your bag can get pretty heavy when you have all those briefs and other work-related things you need."

"I actually carry two bags, one for work and one personal."

"So you're already carrying a lot on a regular basis. You may be experiencing some shoulder and back pain as a result of that, right? Do you ever remove any items so you're not carrying such heavy loads?"

"Unfortunately," I sighed. "That's why I get massages regularly. And sure, I adjust my bag accordingly."

"We all have a choice as to what we keep in our bags, but also how heavy they are. So imagine you're not only carrying your work and personal bags, but you're also carrying your trauma bag. This means you have even more baggage, right? The worst thing about this is that because you've been carrying this baggage for so long, you're used to the pain. You don't even feel it as pain anymore."

"What's your point, doc?"

"So what's my point? My point is that just like you have the choice to carry what you want in your favorite bag, you also have the choice to let go." She posed like Malcom X deep in thought then asked, "If you could fill your personal bag with other essentials, what would they be?"

My mind went blank as I wasn't sure what those items would be. "Probably more water."

"Water is an essential item, so good response," she chuckled. "What if you could carry awareness, kindness, patience, and appreciation? Trust, vulnerability, boundaries, and acceptance? Oh, and my favorites, love, grace, peace, compassion, and empathy?

"Sounds like a heavy bag, Doc."

"No, actually it's the lightest bag you'll ever carry. Imagine the balance you'll feel. Ultimately, Faith, it is very necessary to let go and let in people and things that actually benefit you."

"Like Nicholi," I shook my head in disbelief at myself. "I've been hurting him all this time and didn't even know it."

"First, be kind to yourself. You only did what you know. Secondly, give yourself some credit. You've been married all this time and he hasn't left your side. That means you're doing something right."

She made absolute sense. "Okay, you've got me thinking that you're right. And you are, of course."

"All right, this car is moving," she clapped four times for effect. "I've got an assignment for you. We're going to take a page out of creative arts therapy. The Art Institute has a Picasso exhibition running. That could be a nice family trip, Faith."

"I'm not introducing my brother to another womanizer. But I will find something to do before our next session."

"Fair enough. Just do something that not only relaxes you, but also brings you joy. And remember, choose your bag and your load."

CHAPTER 20
ROLLING HILLS

Cat watched us most of the afternoon. Pat and I took her, along with Eli, my five-year-old niece, Hope, and our husbands, to an arcade park. She tried not to stare, but she couldn't help herself. She circled us like a hawk. Staying close like a shadow, but keeping her distance like the sun. I don't think she's used to seeing siblings having so much genuine fun together. When Pat, Eli, and I were together—without being in our feelings—we just clicked. As always, Pat and I would joke with Eli about being adopted. Then Eli and I would gang up on Pat playing a game of basketball. It never failed that Eli and Pat would team up against me in laser tag. Fortunately, I had Hope with me today. What really had Cat shook was seeing the way our husbands interacted with us. I noticed the quizzical look she gave when Greg and Nicholi paid for everything. Noticed how when either of them conversed with Eli, he not only stood at attention, but also joked around with them. I saw the crease in her brows when Greg playfully stood behind Pat and whispered in her ear during miniature golf. The way Pat lit up and giggled stirred something inside of her. As Eli and Hope played a dance game, I saw the longing in her eyes when my husband pulled me close, pressing his lips to my temple. Cat's gaze followed his hands to my shoulders, then my waist, as if it was the last thing she'd ever see.

I understood how she felt. Growing up, movies and television shows painted pictures of bliss and happy endings. My perfect man was intelligent like Dwayne Wayne, funny like Marlon, no-nonsense like Shazza, handy like Overton Wakefield Jones, and handsome like Morris or Larenz or Marlon, depending on the day. Entertainment love was a stark contrast from my reality.

Completely different from the revolving door of men and women in my family I was advised to call "uncle" or "aunt." I saw strong women yearn for love from the broken men in my family, while the Moore women submitted to infidelity and degradation and shrank their value to revel in a man's. As a child I wondered what kind of man I would end up with. Would I settle for the things I'd always vowed I wouldn't? Would I chase after a man that didn't value what I brought to the table? A man that only saw value in how I could satiate him in the bedroom? Unfortunately, I have done these things. I tried to mold myself into a sexually explicit, ride or die, smart-but-not-smarter-than-him, ego stroking, submissive woman.

It was never enough. I was never enough. I always thought there was something wrong with me. It had to be, because I wasn't pretty enough or thick and curvy enough. I sank into a dark abyss fighting to get someone to love me the way I wouldn't even love myself. I've wondered if my mother has ever felt the same. Seeking comfort in other men's touch, using them as a scratching post to satiate my own unfulfilled yearnings. Pacifying myself during his loud absence, his empty boxes of promises piled up quicker than his lies. I've wondered if my mother has ever felt the same. I learned how to embrace loneliness, which people give such a bad rap. It's only bad when you don't like the person you're with. I learned to value myself. Not everyone deserves to feel the softness of my lips. The gobsmacking tenderness of my body. The snug warmth of my platinum-coated womb. Or be in the presence of my energy. Nina Simone summed it up best: "You've got to learn to leave the table when love's no longer being served." It's easier said than done. But well worth it when you reach the other side.

I want to ask Cat if she ever had a dream man. If yes, did she still think he exists? And if so, does she think she'll ever find him? Instead, I hand her a slice of cheese pizza and strawberry pop. We sit at an outdoor table with Pat and Hope watching the boys race each other in the go karts. We eat in silence, enjoying the warm sun on our faces.

"I'm glad y'all got y'all husbands," she says. "Eli, too."

Pat and I lock eyes as I sip my hot chocolate. It was a chilly Halloween, and we were excited to take Hope trick-or-treating this evening. We smile at our mother. She eats her pizza as if she hadn't said anything.

"You know it ain't never too late for you to be happy," Pat shared. "You gotta start with yourself first, though."

Our phones shake on the table. Their shrewd facial expressions tell me to look at mine.

"Granny being moved again," Pat says. "Let's go."

Out of all the senior homes Granny has stayed in, this one is by far the worst. The hallways wreak of feces. Half the staff is unbothered and the other half is waiting for their shift to end. Shady Pines Senior Living is just that: shady. Granny's medication list has yet to arrive, and Cat has already started cursing staff to hell. It looks like most of the residents sit in the hallway all day. Apparently, it's how they exercise, one of the employees explained. They all look so bored and lifeless. Mainly stare or look down at their feet. I wonder if they'll have Granny sitting out here. If they do, I'm sure she'll try to chat it up with someone and try to play some music. That was her thing: making sure she and the people around her are having a good time. Pat and I made a beeline to Granny's room.

"I wanna go home." Her lunch—a puréed chicken breast with puréed green beans and rice to match—sat stiffer than a bowl of old oatmeal. "This stuff taste horrible. Can one of y'all bring me a burger and a shake? Please, I promise I won't tell anyone."

Her soft eyes swelled my heart. I wished I could give her what she wanted, but she was on a strict diet, per doctor's orders. "As soon as your therapist gives you the okay to eat solid foods again, you know we'll bring you all the foods you want, lady."

Resentfully, Granny ate a spoon of pudding. "If it was y'all in this situation I would give y'all what y'all wanted."

"Now, you know you wouldn't," Pat said. "You'd tell us the same thing."

A loud crash ricocheted through the building. We all look to the hallway. Another loud crash as I stepped into the hall-way. My eyes widened. Randy pulled Nicholi off of Terrell, whose shirt was wet with blood. He wiped at his busted nose. "That was a lucky punch, nigga."

Nicholi strained desperately against Randy, trying to break free from his hold. He spat blood, no doubt tasting the coppery red liquid leaking from his lip. "Put your hands on my wife again, and I'll show you how lucky I am, nigga."

I heard the slight rasp of material ripping as Greg grasped Terrell's shirt to keep him from charging at Nicholi. The two dangerously struggled with each other, almost fighting themselves. I flew toward Nicholi, carefully examining his swollen face. He pulled away, he and Terrell still shouting expletives back and forth to each other. I'd never seen him like this before. Red eyes. Clenched fights. The rise and fall of his chest like harsh waves crashing against a shoreline. He was monstrous.

"Let's go." Randy forced Terrell away. He guided him toward the lobby's door despite his brother's efforts to stay. "You need to cool off, bro."

Nicholi's pounding heart rang in my ears. My feet planted themselves in front of him like roots. "Breathe, baby." He was in another world raging. "Nicholi, please breathe." He rescinded, slowly transforming into the man I recognized.

"I'm sorry." He wouldn't look at me. Shame was written all over his face. His jaw hardened. "The nigga smirked when I saw him and I just lost it."

I wanted to laugh. Yes, because it was the first time I saw my husband truly angry, and in a fight, and he looked sexy as fuck defending my honor. I knew what that took for him to do, so I understood why he felt shameful. My husband is a lover, not a fighter. Obviously, if he felt he had to he would. However, that's his very last reaction. He was considerate.

Thought with logic and spoke with reason. He was hardwired that way. Even when I didn't want him to be. About a year into our relationship, we were driving back to his apartment after a night of dancing. We were in a good mood—laughing, smiling, joking around. I guess we hadn't been paying attention that the light had turned green, so the blinged-out Monte Carlo behind us laid on its horn and swerved ahead of us. The guy was driving way below the speed limit and blasted some whack ass rap song. I was pissed because I know the guy's being a dick, but Nicholi kept telling me to calm down. Finally, the guy reversed into a driveway and pointed a gun at us the entire time. He was wearing too many chains and his dreads were overdue for a touch-up. By that point I was hysterical and pissed because my man hadn't done a thing to defend my honor or his own. Ten minutes later we were parking at his place and I was still fuming that he didn't do or say anything. Before he turned off the engine and left me in the car, he turned to me and said, "We have a future. I want us to live to see it." It took me thirty minutes to swallow my ego before going inside.

I cupped my husband's face as gently as I could. "I appreciate you."

He had no reason to feel ashamed. He protected his family. The woman he loves. Without question I would do the same for him.

CHAPTER 21

HUMAN NATURE

I couldn't stop thinking about Cat at the arcade park. The way she watched us and the things she said. I truly did want her to be happy—with herself and a partner. It's moments like these that I reflect on the good times growing up with her. After all, despite our arduous relationship, I've never thought of her as a villain.

Honestly, my mother was the best part of my childhood. During the summer, she'd take us to Rainbow Beach and the drive-in movie theater. A few of us would hide in the backseat of her truck. She'd pack sandwiches, chips, candy, and pop, and we'd sit on the hood and have a ball. During the winter, she'd take us downtown on Michigan Avenue to see the Christmas lights at Marshall Field's. One year they had a Harry Potter theme, and we geeked out. My best memory by far is her singing, or shrieking by some standards, Mary J. Blige's "Reminisce" to win me tickets to her *No More Drama* tour for my thirteenth birthday. The radio personality told her they were hers if she stopped singing. At the time, I only knew a couple of MJB songs, so I couldn't really jam as the show went on. Cat, however, had the time of her life. She sang along to songs from her diaphragm that brought tears to her eyes, raised her hands to the sky, and reciprocated the energy of a woman letting her know that she wasn't alone. As I looked around the sea of women who mirrored my mother, I pondered what could've possibly happened that made them feel such pain. I wouldn't understand until years later, when I was broken and tears fell from my eyes while listening to MJB's *My Life* album. The catch-22 of it all is that while these women were in pain, there was also a sense of resiliency in the air. These women laughed, danced, embraced each other, and cried tears of joy.

Over the years, I watched Cat remain resilient but exhausted. Trudging through the trenches of whatever came her way. No doubt a generational cycle passed along to her from her mama, which she passed on to me. I come from a long line of strong Black women. We didn't want to be, but we had to. I think it's rooted in us from my Granny's mother, Dorothy, or Dot as she was called. I'd heard plenty of stories about how my great-grandmother had worked hard as a maid to provide for her children. As legend goes, she fled New Orleans after slapping a white woman for disrespecting her. Not long after she arrived in Chicago, she met, fell in love with, and married my great-granddaddy Willie. A tall, charming man, as Granny always described her father. With his flare and Dot's alluring sophistication, they produced children and made a home for them all. Granted, it wasn't always sunshine and rainbows. It was no secret that Granddaddy Willie had a whole other family that lived across the tracks.

I can't fathom the way Dot must have felt about that. I often pondered whether she had ever been out and saw the other woman. If so, did she make a scene? Did she have to affirm herself constantly? Had she ever seen her husband's face in a child while they were out? When he either came home late or didn't come home at all, did she lie in bed wondering if he was loving that woman the same way he did her?

When I was young, sometimes I thought my Granny was mean to my grandfather. I'd only known him as a man doing whatever it took to ensure his woman was happy. It wasn't until I was older, after I heard the whispers about infidelity and drunken nights that sucked the air out of my lungs, that I understood my grandmother had a right to feel whatever she felt. I don't know what that man put her through, but it was enough to make him work daily to regain and rebuild her trust, respect, and love. I've always wanted to ask my Granny: Why did she stay? Was she content, or did she yearn for more? How did she keep it together after all that heartache? Did she have to be still to keep the blazing embers in her belly from spreading throughout her body? And if she was engulfed in a full blaze, did she find her core again after sifting through the embers?

It has been a long journey to forgiving my mother, although the process sped up considerably once I stopped taking things so personally. She is a human being. She is nuanced and multifaceted. She has had experiences, like us all, that have shaped her. Memories that may never see the light of day and secrets that will never reach another's ear. I understand how the hardships of life can drive someone to substance abuse. Couple that with the arduous hardships of dealing with other low-vibrating people, and you'll find that everyone has some sort of vice to get through overcast days. As human beings that is what we do to survive. And it is my mother's human nature that has made me the resilient woman I am today. Just like her mother's did for her and so on and so forth.

The world has stripped Black women of our humanity. And we've conditioned ourselves to strip ourselves even further by allowing so many to continuously mistreat and harm us without consequence. All the while, we continue to extend grace. We continue to pour our energy into people and jobs that aren't even quenching our thirst. We continue to protect people who won't even say our name. We continue to wear masks that we forget to take off because it's easier to appear happy than face the maddening reality of not knowing how to get there. The weight of it all takes a toll, causing knees to buckle. We fall to the floor, and some people never get back up. But there's so much power in it. While it may be the most difficult thing you ever do, imagine the requited love you so desperately desire waiting for you on the other side.

We are human, which means we don't always have it together. So I'm giving my mother some motherfucking grace. She did the best she could. For that, I am grateful.

CHAPTER 22
GET OUT

"You ain't got to leave, Shirley." *Frances frantically followed her sister as she hurried toward the front door.*

Chase paced back and forth in the kitchen talking trash loudly. When he got riled up, he was like a child throwing a temper tantrum.

"I'ma always call it like I see it. I don't care what nobody got to say about it."

Unfortunately, this was a typical scene. Frances would have company over. They'd have a grand old time listening to music, playing card games, and engaging in conversation. One, or all, of her children would come over and join in the festivities. The more truth serum they all drank, the more boisterous they all became. Bodies shimmied in motion, hands slapped each other high fives, and shots of Hennessy were taken like an NBA rookie trying to earn more minutes. Only this time Shirley was the company. And Chase showed up. And because of the liq-

uid courage he drank like water, he decided he would share his
unsolicited opinion with his aunt.

"All I'm saying is, don't keep talking about it if you ain't
gonna do nothing. Nobody wanna keep hearing all that."

Frances tried to rein in her son with a hard stare. It was no
use. It only ignited him more.

"What? She steady talking about the same thing. What them
people say, uh, doing the same thing over and over is insanity."

"Nobody was talking to your motherfucking ass. This grown
folk conversation so get the hell away from me."

"I'm a grown man and I ain't got to go nowhere."

Shirley gathered her things to leave. "You right. I'ma go
before I have to put my foot in your narrow ass."

Frances slammed the door shut behind Shirley. Her walk
just as fierce as her shining eyes.

"That's my sister," she told her son. "Don't you ever speak
to her like that again. She always got my back and I'ma always
have hers."

As the calendar pages continued to flip forward, Aunt Shirley
was pretty mum. She came and visited her sister, and oftentimes left when one of us came to relieve her. It was odd. She
was fidgety, nonjovial, and curt. I chalked it up to her seeing
her big sister in an unsavory light. It was hard on all of us,
and it would've been rude of me to assume that she wouldn't
feel the same. One afternoon, we waited for Granny to return
from playing bingo. Shirley appeared more unnerved than
usual. She sat by the window, angrily knitting a scarf.

"I just can't figure out why y'all would turn her over to the
state," she fumed.

Cat spat her water out onto the floor. "What you talking about?" I saw the steam starting to blow from her ears.

"This senior home for short-term and long-term living," Shirley explained. "Frances on the long-term side. Y'all don't know that?"

The vein on the left side of my mother's neck protruded—code for shit just got real. Everything was a blur from there. Cat was a whirlwind as her words left a trail of destruction in their wake. She summoned a nurse to confirm what her aunt said. It was true. Terrell had signed Granny over. The good news, however, was that we had time to remove her before his decision became permanent. The bad news was that we only had three days to do it.

Back at the house, the family gathered to discuss what the best option would be for Granny. Cat argued that it made sense for her to come back home.

"If she come home we all have to help out," she noted. "This ain't a one-person job."

"That's right," Shirley chimed in. "Ain't gonna be no excuses. So y'all need to be sure this what y'all wanna do."

This was a really unfortunate situation. We all knew that wherever she moved to required constant care. And no matter how much they loved their mother, I knew they didn't want to have that responsibility.

"Let's just bring her home," Chase said. "She only gone be here till the university got an open bed. They say it might take about a month."

The dullness in my chest pulled me toward the kitchen. I grabbed a bottle of water out of the fridge, wishing it was cognac. Nicholi must've sensed my energy because he joined me not long after.

"Come here."

Burrowing my face into his neck, I inhaled his fresh scent. It was the pick-me-up I needed after all that happened that day. I pressed against his hard body, hooking a few fingers into his pants pocket. He placed my hands on his rhythmic heart.

"We're gonna get through this together," he assured me.

When we first met, I used to think this type of shit was corny. I wasn't used to emotionally available and mature men. Couldn't comprehend men that were consistent and honest. Didn't trust men who made me feel pretty without wanting something in return. With Nicholi, I learned to be present instead of waiting for the other shoe to drop.

"I'm surprised y'all ain't had no babies yet with all the lovey-dovey shit y'all do." Shirley leaned against the countertop, stretching her legs out in front of herself. For a sixty-five-year-old woman, Shirley was in incredible shape. "Kids are a beautiful thing," she said, refilling her cup. "When you gonna let him shoot up the club, baby? Shit, if he ain't doing it already," she laughed.

"Kids?" I looked at Nicholi quizzically.

"I've been waiting on you," he said matter-of-factly. "Let's do it."

My body tingled at the thought of starting a family. Damn. I guess I wanted this more than I realized. Nicholi would make a wonderful father, and seeing him in action would be nothing less than beautiful. Then a sinking feeling hit my stomach. Of course, this wasn't the right time to start a family; it was too stressful. But shit, when was the right time? I looked at my husband's excited eyes. He was giddy. We'd make it work.

CHAPTER 23

HOME SOUR HOME

"Eli, we're almost at the house," Faith reassured him. She eyed him in the rearview mirror as she drove. A smile crept up on her lips as she watched her cute little brother. He was so inquisitive at six years old, asking a million and one questions that she tried her best to answer.

"Faye, why birds fly?"

Her heart seemed to freeze, then pound whenever she heard his sing-song voice. "Well, it's just the way they were created. They can fly wherever they want, whenever they want."

Eli flapped his arms as if he was flying and leaned as far as he could to look out the window. His booster car seat added height to his tiny frame. "Even to Granny's house?"

Faith burst into laughter. "Yes, even there."

He strained against his seatbelt then tried to unfasten it. He gave up shortly thereafter. His cheeks flushed red and his eyes began to water. "Hey, when we get to the house you can look to the sky for birds, okay?"

Eli looked to the window again. "Okay," he whispered.

Faith eyed him in the rearview mirror. She couldn't bear to see him sad for any reason at all. It was silly, but she would cry whenever he did. All she ever wanted to do was make him happy. "I have an idea. Let's play I Spy."

He perked up in the backseat. "Me first, me first!" He exclaimed. He looked out the car window as they approached the bridge around the way from the house. "I spy . . . Mama."

Faith looked to where her brother pointed with excitement and saw their mother standing outside of a corner store. She forgot this was one of her mother's favorite places to hang. Faith pulled over to where she was. As she rolled down the window, her mother sauntered over in worn jeans and a T-shirt too small for her. The bags under her eyes said she was tired, and her glassy eyes said she was high.

Faith gripped the steering wheel tight. Eli yelled from the backseat, "Hey Mama!"

She squinted her eyes, realizing it was her children who had stopped. "Hey baby, you been good?"

Eli eagerly nodded his head. "Right, Faye?"

Faith thought about rolling the windows down so Eli could hug her, but saw that he wasn't, per usual, on his mother's mind. She looked at every car that passed. A gray truck pulled up behind Faith's car. A middle-aged man waved his hand out his window.

"I gotta go," she said, walking off. Faith pulled away, watching her mother get into the car. She felt so embarrassed that Eli had to see that, even if he didn't understand what was happening. She checked out her little brother in the rearview mirror again. He lazily meddled with the zipper on his jacket.

"I wish I was a bird so I could fly Mama home."

If only it could be that easy, Faith thought.

If the first week of having Granny back at home was any indication of how things would be, I knew it would be pretty shitty. Pat tried to put together a schedule so that everyone would have a rotating shift, but that quickly fell through the cracks. However, everyone did want to show up together and sit and chat and eat. That was the one thing we could all count on.

"Let her do it herself," Chase had said with impatience yesterday as if he was the one who'd had a stroke that left one side of his body paralyzed. As if it was now his life that was in shambles. His abrasiveness was befuddling. When she sat in her wheelchair, he tried to get her to stand. When it was time for her to eat, he was certain she could use her right hand to feed herself, even though she was still weak from the lack of consistent therapy.

It reminded me of when Aunt Whitney was sick when I was in high school. She had returned home after another hospital stay. She cried. A lot. Granny and Granddaddy did everything they could to ensure that she was comfortable, but their efforts proved futile some days. Once, Granny called me into my aunt's room to help her change her. I shook like a leaf as I grabbed the white bed linen, pulling it as tight as I could, to help maneuver Auntie so Granny could grab her soiled bedding. Weighing less than a hundred pounds, I wasn't very useful for heavy lifting, which is why Mama was called in to take my place. Auntie wailed in pain. Her voice scaled the walls as she kept saying, "Pray for me." I wanted to be there for her. Show her that I was strong. That I loved her. Instead, I retreated back to the dining room table. Watching the tears fall down to my ears in the diamond-shaped mirrors. That would become my permanent position. I'd sit at that table and listen to her moan in pain. At least I heard her. Others walked past that door as her moans fell on deaf ears.

"How you doing, Mama?" Randy popped a chocolate mint. Granny looked upset. Watching them eat those mints likely made her unhappy. Quite frankly, watching anyone eat anything upset her. Chase didn't seem to notice. He popped those mints like popcorn.

"I'm okay," she said, frowning at her oldest son. "At least until the man comes to try and hurt me."

"What man?" Chase said.

Granny peered around the room as if someone lurked in the corners. "He come when I try to go to sleep. He try to hurt me." Granny clutched her chest where her heart was. She fashioned her fists on top of each other, twisting and pushing them into her heart with an agonizing look. "He broke a bottle and stabbed me in my chest. Right here," she said, pointing. She looked at her hands and shirt as if they carried blood stains. "I started screaming, but by the time Cat came, it was too late."

Randy hugged his mother. "I'm sorry I wasn't here, Mama. I won't let him get you again."

Chase waved her off. "Aw, she'll be all right. The doctor said the medicine could make her hallucinate." He turned to Granny. "Ain't no man."

Granny's tears flowed like a waterfall. "Y'all don't believe me? He tried to kill me. Y'all ain't gonna believe me until I'm dead and gone."

"Stop being dramatic. The man ain't real, Mama," Chase said. "All we gotta do is change your medication, so stop all that noise."

I can remember being beyond bored in elementary school. To be fair, a school-wide reading comprehension test showed that I was reading on a college level, so I wasn't engaged or challenged by the curriculum at all. While everyone else took the entire class period to read chapters or take a test, I was often done in ten or twenty minutes. I'd pass the remaining time by scribbling my name and doodling in my notebook, pondering why I had to learn about half-truths and flat-out lies.

Everything I was taught was centered in whiteness. According to our tattered textbooks, our world, for the most part, was what it was because of them. It seemed as if they invented everything and, apparently, could represent everyone. When we learned about people of color, especially African Americans, the few pages were only a speckle in our dense books. Granted, we had Black History Month. So we learned that Martin was peaceful and Rosa sat and Malcom was radical and Mae Jamison was the first African American in space and the typical other facts we were taught every year during this "special" time. Why couldn't we learn about the Tulsa Massacre, Rosewood, and other Black towns destroyed? Or learn about the Black communities that were now modern-day Atlantises: Oscarville, Henry and McKee Islands, Seneca Village? Why couldn't we learn about the New York City draft riots or James Hemings, enslaved chef of Thomas Jefferson, who popularized many staples in American food, including ice cream, macaroni and cheese, French fries, and meringues? Why couldn't we learn about Henrietta Lacks's immortal cells that were stolen without her knowledge or consent—and their profound impact and benefit to medical research? Representation matters, be it through those teaching in the classrooms or the content taught. I am positive that if I had learned that a Black woman's continually dividing cells were invaluable to medical science—today HeLa cells are the preferred human cell line of choice for biomedical research, contributing to medical breakthroughs like the polio and HPV vaccines, chromosome counting, genome mapping, and much more—I would have looked at myself in the mirror differently. But times have changed. Now people are making certain histories more palatable in education textbooks or simply advocating for them not to be taught at all. What a shame it is to live in a country that doesn't acknowledge your humanity. What a shame it is to live in a country that refuses to allow you to be your authentic self.

"How is this my fault?"

Cat stood in the middle of the living room wearing her tight-lipped, nose-crinkled look. Her stance firm with her hands on her hips. Pat, Granny, and I sat at the dining table, our eyes roving back and forth over the thousand-piece puzzle we'd spent the past hour working on. A sullen Eli sat on the stairs. He'd been suspended from school for two weeks for fighting. Again.

"You ain't never got time for the boy," Granny said, handing Pat a puzzle piece. The lioness we were putting together was finally starting to take shape. "I don't know what's wrong with y'all parents today. Y'all act like ain't nothing y'all fault. Y'all complain about what the teachers ain't doing, but you responsible for your child education, too. We already know that the books are old and that all the truth ain't there. We know that some of them people don't care, can't relate, so they don't understand. The people who do care are doing the best they can. But it's also your job, Cat, to look after this boy. You gotta help educate him. You gotta stand up for him and protect him 'cause you know it's stacked against these kids. That mean you gotta be present. That mean you gotta give this boy stability. What, you thought you could have a child and live your life without him in mind? He ain't ask to be here. None of these kids ever do. This stuff starts at home, baby."

"I'm doing the best I can, Mama."

"Are you? And that's one of those questions you ain't gotta answer." She turned to Eli: "And you, come here, baby." Eli stood next to Granny and she put her arm around his waist. "I know you got a lot of anger in you, honey. You growing up, trying to find your way, and you ain't getting what you need from your parents. It ain't right, but we all been there. Listen here: People gonna always try to test you and they always gonna have something to say. You gotta learn to not let that stuff bother you and walk away. You better than that, you hear? If you know who you are, can't nobody tell you different."

"Yes ma'am," he said. "But I don't need people thinking I'm a punk. If they wanna go at it, I'm gonna show them these hands."

It was in this moment I realized that I never could save my brother. He had to save himself if he wanted to live a better life. Granny must've been thinking the same thing.

"You gotta live your life, honey," she said. "Don't make it hard on yourself. It's all fun and games until ten, twenty, thirty years from now and you ain't got nothing to show for it. You gotta responsibility here, too. We can give you the tools you need, but it's your choice to listen and use them. So let's make a deal. We all gonna uplift you, encourage you, support you, stand by you, and love you. But none of that don't mean nothing if you don't believe it. It don't mean nothing if you don't hold yourself accountable. And it don't mean nothing especially if you don't love yourself or think you're worth it. So we'll keep showing up for you if you show up for yourself. We got a deal, baby?" She smiled wide at her youngest grandchild.

"Yes ma'am."

CHAPTER 24

LOVE ON THE BRAIN

The shaking started not too long ago. Dr. Porter said it was a side effect of Granny's medications. Although her body was aimless, she was pointed in all of her decision-making. Even though the right side of her body was paralyzed, her brain led her to believe that she could still operate in the same manner she always had. In her mind, she could stand and walk and roll and even hopscotch if she wanted to. All she needed was a little help to do so. I'd spent the past hour obliging all of Granny's requests in her effort to get out of the wheelchair she felt trapped in. Things had gotten to the point where she adamantly suggested we use the small Hoyer lift in the corner to get her in the bathroom. It was only used to get her in and out of bed and her wheelchair.

"If we can do that, I can take it from there, little lady," she'd said.

I knew it wouldn't work. Yet here we were, trying. I knew our efforts were futile, while she was giving it all she had. I was out of breath trying to hoist her into the lift. Then the outer wheels of her chair got stuck in the door jambs, thwarting our quest. Although now she was nodding off, her perseverance to get through the door to look into the mirror and put her favorite lipstick on before her children arrived was as strong as ever.

"Just bring that lift over here and I'll get in it."

She smiled her crooked smile and I wished I could transform into the Hulk so that I'd be strong enough to carry her myself. Instead, I pushed her back into the living room and grabbed a small mirror and her favorite lipstick.

"Baby, we can't get you into the bathroom because your wheelchair won't fit. Plus, the Hoyer lift can only be operated by someone who knows how—and you know I don't." Her bottom lip quivered like a child who was just told no. "I'm truly sorry I can't do it. But what I can do is hold this mirror while you put this fabulous lipstick on. This way you'll get a better close-up look."

She thought it over, and soon her tense shoulders relaxed. "Thanks, little lady," she said.

Watching Granny put on her lipstick transported me back to when I was seven years old. I would sit doe-eyed on the toilet seat, my two front teeth missing, my head full of colorful ponytails, watching as she applied her makeup. Sometimes she did a full face. Oftentimes, she said, it wasn't necessary. "We're a family of beautiful women, little lady," she explained once. "We only need to enhance our features."

I nodded my head in awe as if I truly understood what she was saying. My mouth hung open as she went through her process: exfoliating her face and then massaging a small amount of coconut oil into it. She'd apply her mascara ever so slowly. Finally, she'd dig through her purse until she found her signature red lipstick.

It dawned on me that this was where the women in our family got their love for all things beauty. At some point or another, I'd had the privilege of watching my mother, aunts, cousins, and sister apply their own rites of passage. I quickly learned that the possibilities were endless. And most important, it all boiled down to how you felt. For me, I only wore a full face when it was some big event. Other than that, I stuck to Granny's simple tradition.

"Are you enjoying being home instead of the hospital, lady?" I asked, watching her press her lips together just like she had when I was seven. Once she smiled at the mirror, I knew she was pleased.

"I sure am," she beamed. "I get to see my sister every day. People come and visit me and sneak me the good food when you ain't around."

"Who? Now you know you're on a liquid food only diet. You gotta take this seriously."

"You know Pat and your mama trying to give me a bath? I told them to get me a chair 'cause the only person bathing me is my man."

A sharp rap on the door kept me from expressing my surprise. Shirley and Shanice strolled in.

"I had to go get her ass before her and Took killed each other," Shirley said. She took one look at her sister and chuckled. "You talking about Charles, huh? I know that look, honey."

Granny blushed. "I was just about to tell Faith about the baths he would run me. Honey, that man would bathe me, carry me out the tub, dry me off, and then oil me down. After that—" she started to continue, then paused. "No, let me stop."

"Nope, lady, spill it." Shanice looked like a kid grateful to finally be at the adult's table.

"There would be huge plush pillows on the floor, candles, and wine. He'd lay me down in front of his fireplace and make me feel . . ." Granny stared off into what only could be Memory Lane.

"Well, they ain't call the motherfucker Bow Leg Charlie for no reason. He was a damn freak. And ain't nothing wrong with that child, okay."

"That's how Took is," Shanice said, smiling wide. "He most definitely be making me feel."

"It just ain't about how he make you feel in the sheets," Granny sighed, "and that's half the battle, 'cause a lot of women don't even feel nothing then. How you feel now? Your face is all red and swollen. Makeup all messed up so that means you been crying. You gotta leave that man alone, baby. Focus on them kids and yourself."

Shanice sat beside Granny, her face in her lap. Granny rubbed her granddaughter's back as if she could restore her energy, time, and youth.

"I done gave him everything," Shanice moaned, "and he keep cheating on me."

"You gotta save something for yourself," Granny cooed. "He will take everything from you if you let him."

Shanice had been with Took for as long as I could remember. Yes, he was charismatic. Yes, he was a looker. Yes, he knew his away around the bedroom. But what good was that if he was community dick? What good was that if he was transparent but not vulnerable? What good was that if he wasn't willing to do anything? His name was fitting because all he ever did was take. When they met, he already had two kids.

Shanice had none. Shanice had an associate's degree in dental hygiene. Took had a GED. After she got pregnant the first time, they moved in together. She paid the bills and he drove her car. All these years later, and it's a classic case of a high-level woman taking care of a low-level man.

"When y'all was growing up, I told y'all not to play house with men who don't wanna make a home with you, or don't know how and ain't trying to learn."

"That's right," Shirley chimed in. "Them motherfuckers ain't stupid. They gonna do what they wanna do. Ain't no use having a man if he gonna ask you for money. Ain't no use having a man if he can't help around the house. Ain't no use having a man if he don't respect you. And it definitely ain't no use for a man if you gotta share his ass with everybody else."

Aretha sang in the background about how she couldn't see herself leaving and Shanice seemed to register the same thought. Her dark eyes were a tunnel that, I'm sure, could be walked for days. She didn't have to utter a word for me to understand. You want that special someone to be there, but they are never present. But you stay because you don't want to be alone. Even though he isn't holding you at night. Even though he isn't fucking you right. Even though he only tears you down. It's draining. Constantly pouring into someone who only receives and for damn sure isn't reciprocating. Eventually you become a well run dry. And even then, you try to conjure up whatever little you have left to satiate his thirst. All in the hopes that things will fall into place and he'll not only see your worth, but act on it. Because if he did, he'd treasure you. Appreciate you. Love you. Keep you safe. Right?

"I know it ain't easy to leave," Granny said, "but it's the first step to get to the other side. We all gotta choice in the life we live and how we live it. You can sacrifice, but don't settle. He keep showing you he ain't ready. You've given this man enough grace, now go get yours."

"I got these kids."

"What that mean? They don't drop your value, baby. And any man that thinks so is stupid."

My cousin sat in disbelief. She couldn't see the forest for the trees.

"You got a degree," Shirley noted. "A good job cleaning people mouths and shit. I know you got good credit. You're smart. You'd stay beautiful if you'd stop letting that man put his hands on you. You got more going on for yourself than Took and majority of these fools out here. And you best believe they know it." She poured her drink into a glass.

"Why you always drink out of a glass, lady?" Shanice watched our aunt pull a pack of straws from her purse. It was no secret that Shirley drank only out of glasses, never plastic cups. And if you tried to give her one there was hell to pay.

"'Cause I'm worth it," she replied, incredulous. "Ain't you worth it? You worth so much more, baby. You deserve so much more than you allowing. Look at Faith. You can find a good man like Nic. That man is beautiful and treats this girl over here like Queen Mother."

"Ain't no man like that gonna want me."

With the exception of Granny, who could only drink water, Shirley handed us cups as well. I took one sip and frowned at the cognac. I needed an ice cube or something.

"I thought the same when I met Nicholi," I explained. "But I'm glad he proved me wrong. He's a really good man. And I just stopped fighting him. One of the best decisions I've ever made."

"Yeah, you was rough, little lady," Granny chuckled. "I remember when you first brought him home. The poor boy brought this child some flowers and she threw them in the garbage."

"You should've whooped her motherfucking ass, Frances," Shirley said, sipping her drink.

"I remember the flowers," I said in my defense. "I don't remember throwing them away."

"I told him you ain't know no better but you would learn," Granny recalled. "Now look at you. Man got you glowing like the North Star."

I thought back to all the reckless shit I used to do when Nicholi and I started dating. I didn't take him seriously. I didn't respond to his texts or phone calls immediately. Self-sabotage and projection were my favorite things. My appreciation ran deeper for him more than words could express.

"I'm grateful," I said. "But don't get it twisted, because he's glowing, too."

Shirley threw her cup in the air for a toast, "I heard that."

"We see that," Granny said. "But he was ready and you wasn't. You saw his actions matched his words and then you fell in line, right, little lady?"

"I did. Still getting better too. I've been thinking a lot about what I want from marriage."

"It ain't easy, but it's all a choice, baby." Shirley poured herself another drink. "It's a lot easier submitting to a man that's showing you can trust him."

CHAPTER 25

SHARP OBJECTS

"Can you do something for me please, Faith?" Granny sat up in bed, her eyes glued to the television. "I sure would like that Memory Pillow. It's supposed to be so soft and comfortable and remembers the mold of your head."

I checked out the TV Every other day this woman saw something she wanted. "You want something that remembers the mold of your head?"

"If it help me sleep better, yes." Granny nudged Pat, who was preparing her morning medicine. "You know they sell them at Walmart. That's where you going, right?"

"Yes, I'll get you one."

It was Thanksgiving Day, and I needed to hit the stores early if we wanted to get a start on preparing Granny's first puréed home-cooked holiday meal. Granny's phone buzzed. The caller ID said it was Shanice. Granny's nose wrinkled as soon as she heard her granddaughter's voice.

"It's a shame y'all won't come see me. I ain't seen you since last month."

She put the phone down by her side. This was a new thing for her. Whenever someone called her, she said what she needed to and then put the phone down as if the conversation was over. In her mind, I suppose, there was nothing else to discuss. You were either there for her or you weren't. Period.

"She still on the phone," Pat said. "Talk to her."

This time Granny stared at the phone while she talked. "I'm not happy with you. Come see me and we can talk then." She hung up and went back to watching TV.

"Baby, I know you're upset, but that wasn't nice," Pat said.

"I'm tired of people treating me like this," she pouted. "I done did a lot for all of y'all. I have," she exclaimed as though someone had tried to diminish her impact on all our lives. "Now that I can't help, nobody wanna help me. Nobody come around. I can't walk. This ain't living."

Tears welled up in her once warm eyes and spilled out. I looked her over. Her appearance was gaunt and she barely ate. We couldn't force her to eat, but I was glad she had the feeding tube. It was the only way to guarantee she ate every day, since she wasn't willing to. Honestly, I was surprised she was up talking. She barely responded to anything these days. She lay in bed, rolling her upper body from side to side, staring at her hands or the wall. Or she slept all day. She didn't even respond to her music anymore, which is so tragic I can't even fathom it.

From my earliest days, I remember music having a major impact on my life. I was only five years old when Toni Braxton released her self-titled debut album. You wouldn't have known that, though, by the way I sang "Seven Whole Days." It was my favorite song in the world. How a five-year-old identified with such a song, I couldn't tell you. I was also head over heels with Tony Terry's "When I'm with You," which I sang every time it was played and every time I left my Granny's house. I never wanted to be without music or her.

"I can't even go get Randy a gift for his birthday 'cause I'm stuck in this bed." Granny pounded her bedside rail with her fist. "Will you please get him something while you're out, Faith? Take my card and get him a sound bar so he can play his music, baby, okay? Pat, give my wallet to Faith, little lady."

I looked at my grandmother with overwhelming amazement. Even when she knew she deserved better from people, she still thought of them. Still wanted to do for them and make them feel good. I could only pray that I could one day have that type of unconditional love for others.

"I'll take care of it," Granny said. "And yes, I'm sure. Pat, I've got your list too."

My emotions ran rampant as I shopped the aisles. Everything around me was a blur. I maneuvered numbly through the store, grabbing items with such nonchalance they could have easily slipped through my fingers.

"Breathe."

I turned doe-eyed to see an elderly woman with purple hair wearing a matching purple fur coat. She was fabulous, like the icon that is Diahann Carroll. "Everything will be all right," she said.

With that, she was gone. Her words remained with me as I drove home. The chic lady was right. I rolled my window down and let the wind give me a rush. Let the sun rays warm my face as I unloaded my car and exhaled deeply. I just had to breathe. And remind Granny to do the same despite these unfortunate circumstances. A slight smile on my face, I wondered if I would be able to get everyone over to watch football on Sunday, too. The Bears were playing, and no doubt that'd really cheer up Granny.

And then all I heard was arguing. For some reason, I just knew that my family had nothing to do with this loud cadence taking place. They all understood how grave Granny's situation was. They wouldn't jeopardize her health further for whatever asinine reason they could conjure up. Rounding the corner to the house, my assuredness disappeared just as quickly as a shooting star on a dark night. Chase fled out of the front door like a madman. His eyes wild and his steps so hard it seemed as though he could break the concrete as he walked. Cat followed in hot pursuit while Pat closed the door behind them. I saw the anger in her face, the glossy look of her eyes. She was pissed.

"You kiss my ass," Cat shrieked.

The bulging store bags flanked loose at my sides. I was beyond over this shit. "What the hell is going on?"

"And you can be replaced, too," Chase said accusingly, turning to me in his direct but animated way, "'cause you ain't running a thang either."

My brows furrowed in confusion. *What the fuck's wrong with you now?* is what I wanted to say.

"What's your problem?" I asked instead.

"I ain't gotta go nowhere. It's y'all that can leave since y'all trying to control it all." He lurched toward me. "Y'all ain't doing nothing I can't get someone else to do."

"This your mama too," Cat exclaimed with an intense finger. "You can come and help."

"I done told you that ain't my responsibility. But I got y'all number."

He took off toward his car while Cat stalked into the house like the Big Bad Wolf. I sat the bags on the kitchen counter, looking to Pat for any kind of answer. She only shook her head. Cat went into the bathroom, muttering expletives as she brushed her teeth.

I took a seat beside Granny, whose shoulders dipped toward her chest like tulips without sunlight. "Are you okay, baby?"

"They just don't know when to quit," she said, disheartened. "It's a shame."

My mama rushed out of the bathroom like a quarterback. "No, it's a shame your son don't wanna help," she said, flailing her toothbrush about. Specks of wet toothpaste landed on Pat, and that was the straw that broke the camel's back.

"Y'all can both leave with that mess," Pat pointed toward the door. "I told y'all Granny don't need this added stress."

Cat looked as if she would haul off and slap her. Pat looked like she was daring her to do it. Mama hadn't whooped her since junior high, so I doubted it would happen. Then again, the two had always mixed like oil and water. And anything was possible with all this shit happening lately. Regardless, my money was on Pat because of pure adrenaline.

"Don't trip," Cat grabbed her purse and jacket. She did the one thing she knew how to do best: leave.

Granny was all smiles after dinner. She clung to her bed, fighting sleep, refusing to leave us for dreams. Womack and Womack's "Baby I'm Scared of You" reminded us of the love we didn't want. Terrell and Randy played spades with Took and Shanice. Nicholi twirled Shirley in circles to the funky tune while Eli, surprisingly, kept up with Mama on the dance floor. Pat sang the words of the song as if her husband couldn't hear a thing. I danced with Hope in my arms, teaching her about the kind of love she deserves.

"Let's dance," Spider said, grabbing my elbow.

"Leave me alone," I brushed him off.

"Now why you gotta act like that? You know how we used to do."

"We ain't do shit," I said, handing Hope to Pat. "That was all you."

He smacked his lips. "Stop it. You know you liked it."

"You gonna like me if you don't move around bruh." Nicholi stood inches from Spider, who looked like a runt by comparison. The music stopped briefly in between tracks and then Taana Gardner's "Heartbeat" mimicked my own. Shirley and Cat stood behind their favorite in-law as if he was about to tag them in.

Spider smiled. Terrell waved him to follow as he walked toward the front door. "Maybe next time," he said, following his leader.

"Don't worry about that boy," Shirley said. "Come on y'all, we ain't gonna let him mess up our good time."

Mama poured herself another drink. "That's right."

I caught my husband's curious eyes and we made our way to the bathroom.

"You okay?" He held my shoulders, looking me square in the face.

"Yeah."

"So, are you going to tell me what that was all about?"

I squeezed my eyes shut, exhaling deep. "I've never talked about it. And honestly, I don't see the point in doing so now."

"Faith." My husband kissed each of my eyelids, then caressed my cheeks. "You know you're safe with me," he whispered matter-of-factly.

"My family has been partying for a long time. It seems like when two or more gather, there's always a reason to celebrate. They can drink from sun up to sun down, and the more they drink, well, the less they pay attention to things. When I was in the sixth grade, Terrell had a big birthday bash at the old house in Markham. The grown-ups played their music loud and danced as if it was the last thing they'd ever do. The kids were supposed to be asleep, which we were. But I had to use the bathroom. I tried to keep my eyes closed so I wouldn't lose my sleep, but I knew it was early in the morning because of the light outside our bedroom window.

"When I stumbled into the bathroom, I didn't know he was in there. Before I could leave, he told me to stay and he'd go. He was done, he said. Just finished washing his hands. I didn't think to lock the door because why would I? I'm at home. My eyes were still shut when he made his way back in. I sat on the toilet, nonchalantly telling whoever was trying to come in that I was in there. When I heard the door lock, I opened my eyes. And he was standing their rubbing a bulge in his pants. He asked me if I knew what a dick was. I said no. He unzipped his pants and something fell out that I knew was wrong for me to see. So I turned away. He said if I didn't look he'd tell my mama. So I did. He rubbed himself, telling me that when he was happy his dick got big and nothing bad would happen. He said that when he was really happy, cream came out of it. Then he told me to wipe myself and wash my hands but to give him my panties. He sniffed them as if they carried the best scent in the world and before long the cream he told me about shot out onto his hands."

"Faith—"

"That was the first time," I continued. "One month later he cornered me again. I found out the locks were so weak you could open the door with a butter knife. This time he taught me how to stroke him to make him happy and cream. He left five dollars on the sink and warned me not to tell anyone about our little fun. That went on until the summer I was going to eighth grade."

I looked at my husband. His big brown eyes were alert. Brows furrowed with concern. His breathing even. Measured. Composed. "Anything else you want to know?" I asked.

His mask fell. "I am so sorry that this happened to you," was all he could say as he wrapped his arms around me as tightly as he could. "It's a bit scary how you shared this without any emotion. Have you talked to Dr. Tucker about this?"

"I haven't."

We locked eyes. "Will you?"

I chuckled at the thought. "I know I need to. And I will eventually."

CHAPTER 26

C'EST LA VIE

"You sure you okay, baby?"

Granny had been breathing funny all morning. Well, at least according to Pat. Apparently, it started not long after she had breakfast. I showed up about brunch. I browsed a magazine while Pat watched *The Real Housewives of Atlanta* on her phone.

"I'm okay," she said, turning onto her side. Her hands grasped the rail of the medical bed firmly. Her voice sounded fine, but she kept trying to clear her throat. "I'm okay."

The next few hours passed lazily. While Granny slept, both Pat and I kept a keen eye on her. The sunlight from her bedroom window cast a shining glow over her. She looked peaceful. More peaceful than I'd seen her in a long time. Hopefully, we would all be able to keep that up, especially with her birthday coming in the next couple of months. She never wanted to celebrate her birthday, and the family obliged every year by throwing her a huge birthday party. She would be eighty-one, so I was sure the family would want to put something extra special together for her, especially with everything she's gone through.

"Have you heard anything about planning something for Granny's birthday?" Pat was glued to her phone. The closed captions were on, but she was so into it. I didn't understand how she could watch it, and she couldn't understand how I watched *Braxton Family Values*, so I guess we were even.

"Not yet. But I'm sure it'll come up soon." A beat. "I don't think she up for it, honestly. The past couple of weeks she been different. Talking about how she miss and wish Granddaddy Charles and Auntie Whitney was here. It's like she just over it all."

My eyes zoomed in on Granny. The glow I saw literally came from the sunlight as her skin no longer held its own natural light. In fact, she was a bit pale. Heavy bags under her eyes. Her hair didn't shine as it normally did. I understood why she was unhappy. She was a shell of her former self. She couldn't walk, chew, or swallow solid foods. She couldn't bathe herself or go to the bathroom on her own. She couldn't get up and go wherever whenever she chose to. That's a hard pill to swallow for someone who's lived eighty years. To no longer have her independence. Her freedom. A livelihood. It wasn't surprising to hear her talking about Granddaddy Charles and Auntie Whitney, either. She stood by their sides in their times of need. No doubt they would be by hers if they were here. "I lost my best friends," she would say at the mention of their names. I never heard her say that about anyone else.

"Let's call a family meeting," I said. "We have to be better for her. So whatever she needs, let's make it happen."

"Period," Pat agreed.

Granny stirred in bed. She tried clearing her throat again. I went to her side. "You okay?" She nodded yes. "You sure? Blink if you're not." She didn't blink. Then she closed her eyes and opened them. Was that a blink? No sign of fear in her face or eyes. She wasn't anxious. She looked calm, actually. "Pat, call the ambulance. Let's be sure you're good, lady."

I wiped her forehead. She tried clearing her throat again. No luck. *If she's calm, we should be, too,* I thought. While Pat gathered Granny's purse and items, I sat by her side humming a song and caressing her hair. It was still the gorgeous silver I loved. She was falling asleep again when the paramedics showed. They came in like a blur. Checking her vitals and asking why we called. In no time they had strapped her to their stretcher and were putting her in the ambulance.

"I'll meet you there," Pat said as I hopped in the passenger side of the ambulance. "Let me take a quick shower."

The ride to the hospital was bumpy as hell. I wasn't sure if the streets were horrible or if the ambulance had bad shocks. Either way, I just wanted to get to the hospital as quickly as possible. It was a ten-minute ride that turned into twenty because there was a train sitting on the tracks, which meant we had to go up Halsted Street and go around. As we rushed through all the stoplights, I couldn't help but notice life happening. The madman walking down the street visibly arguing with himself. The liquor stores and fast-food restaurants located every couple of blocks. The garbage littered damn near everywhere. Children coming from God knows where and hopefully heading home. The older woman standing at the bus stop in her work uniform with bags of groceries. A teenage girl with her face buried in her phone, likely perusing social media. Life always goes on.

"You've got a sweet lady here," the paramedic said, pushing Granny through the hospital's emergency room doors. He was short, with dusty blond hair. "It was a bumpy ride, so she spit up a bit on the way here, but I cleaned her up."

I squeezed Granny's hand. It was warm and soft. "Thank you. She's awesome."

The nurses tended to her quickly once she was situated in the room. I rummaged through her purse to get her list of medications. A short, stout woman suctioned her mouth out while I conversed about her medications with the brunette nurse. She looked up from the list and then at Granny.

"Is she always like this? Quiet and staring off?"

Granny stared at the wall. "Yeah, she's been doing this a lot lately." I went to her side and put my hand on her shoulder. "Baby, tell the nurse how you've been feeling."

No response. I shook her shoulder harder. Grabbed her face and looked into her eyes. Blank. Her chest neither rose nor fell. "Come on lady, don't play like this."

Panic-stricken, the brunette nurse took action. "Code blue," she called out. In less than five seconds the room was a whirlwind. Someone put their hands on my shoulders to steer me out, but my feet were cemented to the floor. Nurse Brunette started compressions and Granny flopped like a rag doll. Mouth open and eyes wide. My mind went blank. Ears heard no sound. Body shook and knees buckled until they hit the floor. Someone held me as I bellowed. Squeamish like a fish out of water, I tried to get loose. Tried to get to my baby. Tried to remind her of reasons to live. They pulled the curtain. Then shit went black.

CHAPTER 27

FINALLY HEARD

It's strange. Watching everyone react. Confused eyes seek understanding. Silent thoughts scream judgments and indictments. Now they get it. Now they understand how important she is. Her value. Granny had been fighting for her life. She was fighting for her life when she decided it was time to let adults be adults. She was fighting for her life when she started holding people accountable. She was fighting for her life when she finally decided to choose herself. But life happened.

Screams echoed from Granny's room. A purse flew into the hallway and crashed into the wall. Its contents splayed onto the floor. Cat hurried to pick up her things, cursing someone out at the same time.

"We ain't pulling no plug. God got the last word on this," Chase roared.

Cat viciously wheeled around to face him. "Mama ain't wanna be hooked up on no machine. This ain't what she wanted."

"She'll wake up," Chase said. He shook his head in agreement. It seemed like he was trying to convince himself more than anything. "We just need to pray."

I guzzled my cold bottle of water, wishing I had another to douse my face with. The waiting room was full but eerily quiet. No one had any words. No one wanted to express any doubt. It seemed as if people were trying to keep hope alive. I stretched my short legs out in front of me. Compared to Nicholi's it's almost embarrassing, but more amusing than anything. He wraps an arm around me, kissing my forehead.

"Vault," he says in my ear. He wanted to share something that he didn't want anyone else to hear.

"Yes?"

"We're going to get through this. No matter what happens."

I squeezed his hand. Appreciating his optimism, but at the moment I couldn't see the forest for the trees. It was just too much.

"Did you bring Mama life insurance policy?" Terrell stood in front of me as if he had something better to do. Chase flanked his right, eating sunflower seeds. Randy stood to his left just as calm and patient as always.

I felt my husband's grasp around me tighten. "No."

"Well, why not?" Chase said, shaking the seeds in his hand like dice. "We got things to do and ain't got time to be waiting around on you."

"Granny's papers are in her safe." I exhaled deep. "Plus, neither of you are the beneficiary, so it really doesn't matter."

"See, this ain't what we gone do," Chase said, shaking his head. How you gone tell us we ain't the beneficiary?" He pointed between him and his brothers. By now, all the family was paying attention. Shirley sat crouched around a board game with Pat, Eli, and a few other cousins. You could hear a pin drop.

"Look, Granny changed her beneficiaries a few weeks ago to Randy and Cat. They were there, and Shirley."

Chase and Terrell looked at Randy in disbelief. "So you just wasn't gonna say nothing," Terrell said, turning to his brother.

"Mama told us not to say nothing so I didn't," Randy said.

The water I guzzled hit my bladder. I let Nicholi know I was going to the bathroom and started to make my way. Terrell grabbed my arm. "We ain't done talking."

"Keep your damn hands off of me," I said, yanking away. Flashbacks of our last encounter had my eyes stinging with tears. My body shook with rage.

Nicholi stood erect immediately, taking his place in front of me. Terrell didn't budge as they glared at each other.

"We ain't even on that, bro," Randy said, pushing Terrell back. "We can get them papers another time. It ain't even about that right now anyway."

Chase pushed through his brothers vehemently. "Nah, skip that. This *our* got damn mama. We want them papers today. You ain't got nothing to do with this. Y'all ain't controlling shit." He pointed a skinny finger toward me, Pat, and our mother. "You got an education so you think you better than us? You think 'cause you done went and got a little money you doing something? Y'all the one killing *my* mama."

It was as if something had cracked inside of me and I wasn't certain it was beyond repair. "Your mama? Where have you been Mr. She Ain't My Responsibility? Where were you when your brother kept moving her to all these facilities without ensuring she had therapy or adequate care? Where were you when Pat needed someone to help her with anything with your mama? Getting her to the doctor, making sure she had her meds? Anything? Yes, I am educated. Yes, I have money now. All of which qualifies me to help my grandmother in any way I can. You know why? Because she always did whatever she could for me. And you. And your brothers and my mother, and the whole damn family. So we should all be fucking grateful and thank God that we've had her in our lives."

Nicholi wrapped his arms around me, pulling me into him and away from them. "Time," he said.

"Take a look at where *your* mama is right now and whose fault it really is," I said.

"Time, babe," Nicholi echoed, pulling me out of the waiting room.

I collapsed in his arms. Furious at the things I had just said, but relieved the words had been released.

"It's okay." Nicholi held me tight. "It's okay."

CHAPTER 28

PROFESSING FAITH

"So we gonna have this family prayer call every night until Mama comes home," Chase said. "We know things look bad right now. But we ain't listening to nothing no ordinary man say. This is an extraordinary situation, so y'all know what that mean, right? We gonna need an extraordinary God to fix our problem."

The family murmured on the line. Brenda was damn near shouting and Shirley had let out a series of "that's right." It felt the same as when I'd sit in on presentations: some people were ecstatic to be there while others just wanted it to be over.

"Right, now let's get to it." Randy expeditiously directed his brother back to the task at hand. We had been on the phone for forty-five minutes now. Twenty of which were spent getting everyone on the line. The next fifteen minutes my mama and Terrell spent bickering over who would visit Granny first in the morning. He argued he needed to go early because of work.

"Everybody know you ain't got no job, man," she snorted.

It went up from there. If Shirley hadn't gotten them to calm down, they would still be going at it like cats and dogs. Now, for the past ten minutes, Chase was giving a passionate speech about the importance of family and why we have to stick together in times like these. Pat sighed. I wondered if she was as over his shit as I was. My phone shimmied in my hand. My sister was truly telepathic. Her text read:

Girl I wanna tell him to cut the shit so bad rn.

You and me both, I replied.

Chase cleared his throat like a chair scraping against a hardwood floor. I could imagine him right now in his Sunday best, wearing his Bluetooth. Imagine his hands moving like an orchestra director as he spoke every word with fervor. Imagine the seriousness cascading over him as he stepped to his pulpit via phone. He was home.

"Heavenly Father, we approach your throne tonight as humble servants. You know these are hard times right now. So you know it's difficult to keep going. Some of us feel helpless, Father. Matthew 18:20 says that where two or three gather in your name, you are in their midst. Well, here we are, Father. See, we know it's strength in numbers; that's why we here. We need you to cover our mama, granny, sister, you know who she is to everyone. Cover her from the crown of her head to soles of her feet, oh Lord. Heal her mind and her body, Father. We know that if you so wanted to you could open her eyes and have her walk right out of that hospital door. Here we are at the hem of your magnificent garment, Father, asking that you perform one of your miraculous miracles like only you can. We understand that we are not worthy, but you love us anyway, and that's why we continue to praise your name, Jehovah. We're looking for a testimony, Father. And will tell all paths that we cross that this miracle was at the hands of no one but you. Forgive us where we fall short, Father. In the name of your son, Jesus Christ, amen."

NIGHT VI

"Tonight we magnify your name. Some may call you Lord. Others may call on you as the Son of God or Son of David. They may even call you the Lamb of God. The Light of the World. Even the King of the Jews. But I call you Christ the Redeemer! Ain't nobody ever love me the way you do. You done died for my sins, giving me another chance at life—giving us all another chance. And you know. Our mama, sister, granny needs another chance, too. We are asking for your help 'cause you are the ultimate intercessor, Lord. The scripture tells us that no man can come to the Father without going through you. So here we stand, at the hem of your magnificent garment, with our hands outstretched Lord. Like John 14:16 say, you are the way, the truth, and the life. This is an impossible situation and only you Father can make it possible. We humbly ask that your Father bend a glorious ear to our prayers. We know we are not worthy but my mama is, Lord. And right now she needs help more than ever. Plant your feet and stand strong in the gap for us, oh Lord. For we know that through you all things are possible. Guide us, Lord. Keep your loving arms wrapped around Mama. We ask these things in your name, Jesus Christ, amen."

NIGHT XI

"Father, tonight we are prostrated before your glorious throne. Our mother, sister, grandmother, Frances is under attack. These doctors saying they don't know why she bleeding and they can't stop it. They saying it's a shortage of her rare blood type. They saying the tube is doing all the work and it ain't looking good. Well, you know what I told them people? You must not know my God."

"They don't know Him," Shirley lamented.

"Isiah 54:17 warns us that the enemy comes to steal, kill, and destroy," Chase continued. "You know what else he told us? He told us that no weapon formed against us will prosper. We know that Yahweh will spite every tongue that speaks ill of one of His children. And we all know that Frances loves her some Jehovah. You know why? 'Cause she know she couldn't walk this life alone. And Father, we know we can't, either. That's why we here asking you to protect Frances. We know that if it is your will you can stop her bleeding. If it's your will you can supply a surplus of her rare blood type, and if it's your will, you can most definitely restore her breath to where she can sit up and remove that tube herself, oh Lord. Yes, we know these things because you are a God that specializes in the impossible. You parted the Red Sea and led your people to safety. You sent manna to your people when they were hungry. You restored Jeroboam's withered hand and cured Naaman of leprosy. I could go on and on about your wonderful works, Father, because there is no limit to your mercy and grace. We just humbly ask that you extend that overflow to Frances, oh Lord. As always, we give you all the glory, all the praise, and ask these things in Jesus's name, amen.

NIGHT XVII

"Tonight we gonna take our time, y'all," Chase smiled through the phone. We gonna take our time like Mama do when she cooking that baked macaroni and cheese. We gonna take our time like she do when she looking for a certain song. And you know we gonna take our time like her when she mixing that delicious drink now. You know who else take His time?"

"Tell me who," Shirley exclaimed.

"Jehovah God. He took his time when he created earth. Y'all know it's some beautiful places on this earth. You got Table Mountain in Africa and them rainbow mountains in China, the Blue Lagoon in Iceland, and countless other breathtaking natural wonders all over the world. Jehovah is the ultimate creator, and He took His time. So that mean we gotta be patient and wait on him. Ain't that what Psalm 27:14 tell us to do? See, people don't know how to just chill today. Why, you ask? Because everybody want things fast, real quick. They wanna heat up they mac and cheese in the microwave.

"That shit ain't right," Shirley said. "What? Y'all know it ain't."

"We know what you mean, Shirley, because it ain't right. But that's okay 'cause we know better. These doctors running they tests, looking at they scans, and coming to they own conclusions. That's fine and well because we need their help. But we know that ain't got the final word. They gonna be done with they stuff. But Father, we know that you have the last word. We know that you can see what's wrong and can fix it in an instant. We just waiting on you to show us what you gonna do because you have the last word. You are the Alpha and the Omega and the creator of unmatched beauty. There is no one greater, Father. This is why we give you all the praise, all the glory, and will continue to magnify your name. Thank you for keeping us going, Father. In the name of your son, Jesus Christ, amen."

NIGHT XXIV

"Our hearts are weary tonight, Father. Many of us feel beat down, but we continue to march on like those who circled around the walls of Jericho until its bricks came tumbling down. Yes, we are thirsty and need water. Yes, our bodies and minds are tired and we need rest. Yes, our flesh is weak and we need to be strengthened because these dark days seem endless. But we are still, Father. We are waiting on you. Philippians 4:6 reminds us to be anxious for nothing, but in everything by prayer and supplication and thanksgiving to let our requests be made known to you. You know that our hearts desperately desire Frances to get better and come home. And we know that we have to be patient because you are an on-time God. Ain't that right? He may not come when you want Him to, but He's always on time. See, we know that you are in the mist, Father, because we are gathered here in your name. So, we just want to praise you tonight for quenching our thirst. We want to thank you for the food that we eat daily to nourish our bodies. We want to thank you for the comfortable beds we sleep in at night when we are able to shut our minds off from the abyss of thoughts running through our minds. We glorify your name, Jehovah, for waking us up every day, for allowing us to get to where we need to safely and unharmed, and getting right on back home when we done. It ain't easy to see our mama Frances like this, but with you in our corner, we know that she's in the best hands. You created the heavens and the earth. Father, you commanded the sea and the ocean to never mix. You gave us our Lord and savior Jesus Christ, who died for our sins. We know that nothing is possible without you, Father. That's why we will continue to magnify you and your name, Jehovah. We know that we are unworthy but ask that you continue to keep your loving arms around us and Mama especially right now. We ask these things in the name of your son, Jesus Christ, amen."

NIGHT XXXIII

"People pointing fingers and talking a whole lot of nonsense right now, Father, but we ain't listening to them. You know my heart and what I been doing for my mama. So I ain't gonna let nobody make me feel bad. Talking all that nonsense, we ain't trying to hear all that, Lord. Nah, we ain't hearing that noise. I been fasting so you can guide me and my brothers and sister to make the right decision for our mama. I been fasting so you can help me get some inner peace in my mind, body, and soul, Father. I been fasting so your will can take place, oh Lord. 'Cause this is about my mama. I know, just like they know, in James 2:17 that faith without works is dead. So they need to worry about what they doing or ain't doing. But what them doctors talking? They can get on somewhere. We already know that what they can do is limited. See, they only flesh and blood. Mama's situation is supernatural, so we need a supernatural being like you, Father. This is an impossible situation, but we know that's what you specialize in, so we at the right place, Father. We know we on your time and we can't do nothing about it. We ask that you help us to trust one another and help keep each other strong. Because that's how we gonna get through this as a family. We ain't gonna let the enemy divide and conquer us. We all we got. So Lord, please strengthen us and help us to get on the same page. We ask all these things in the name of your son, Jesus Christ, amen."

NIGHT XL

Randy stood in the middle of his mother's living room with clouded eyes. In all my years of knowing my uncle, I had never seen him cry or show any emotion. He had spent much of his life in prison, and when he was home he spent much of his time in the streets. Randy was my favorite uncle, though. He had a gentle spirit, never raised his voice, and if you asked him to help with something, he made himself available. When I left for college, everything was planned except how I would get there. Randy took me. When I told Granny I was short on cash for books, Randy gave it to me. When I came home at the end of the semester and he saw how heartbroken I was, he offered to take care of it.

"Give me his address and I'll send some guys to see him. I promise you he'll apologize."

I told him none of us needed that karma, but I appreciated it. Now my uncle stood with his mask off and veil lifted, showing emotion that I never knew he was capable of.

"This is the best way I can break this down," he said. "I found out today Mama is in a coma state. The doctor say she suffering. I think she is, too. Why would we keep her on this breathing machine if everything breaking down?" He turned and looked each and every one of us in the face. "Her heart breaking down. Her lungs failing. Her kidneys is shot. And when they take that breathing tube out the people say she gonna stop breathing. I ain't trying to act like I don't care, because I do, but this is the truth.

"I just want y'all to know what's really going on. They say if we take her home she won't have a good quality of life. Y'all know Mama ain't want that. And you know what? I think she at peace. It was like she was resting while I was there. And if she was woke and could talk I know she would've told me to go," he smiled. "She resting. That's what I believe. Again, I care about my mama and I love her. But that's how I feel and I don't want her to suffer. We all gotta think about her. We are prolonging the inevitable. If God is gonna raise her up, He will. There ain't no doubt about that."

After forty nights of prayer, the family was weary. The living room tingled with heat and sighs, and grumbles bounced from wall to wall. Looks of defeat collided and clashed with looks of fervor and an unwillingness to let go. We were divided, per usual.

"I agree," Chase chimed in, clasping his brother's shoulder. "It's out of our hands now. It's up to Jehovah. So, we need a vote. They're gonna take the tube out and try to do a tracheotomy. If her heart stop, who in favor of not having the doctor resuscitate Mama?"

"How about if her heart stops, they can try to resuscitate her? And if they can't, we go from there?" Shirley reasoned.

Heads bobbed in agreement around the room.

"It's all in his hands now," Chase said, stepping to his pulpit. "All we can do is stay prayerful and faithful. We have to acknowledge and surrender to his will. Like Randy said, if He gonna raise her up, He will. We just have to let His will take place. Everybody bow your heads as we step to the throne.

"Father, this is the time to exercise faith. Deuteronomy 31:6 says be strong and of good courage, do not fear or be afraid of them; for the Lord your God, He is the one who goes with you. He will not leave you nor forsake you," he said as his voice cracked. "We need you more than ever right now, oh Lord. Here we are standing in the gap, Father. Asking for your will to take place. Like 2 Corinthians 4:18, we are fixing our eyes not on what is seen, but what is unseen, since what's seen is temporary, but what we can't see is eternal. Like Elijah, we have consistently prayed for the health and recovery of our mama, sister, grandmother, Frances. We will continue to march like Joshua and the people who marched around the walls of Jericho, oh Father, until the walls of this sickness that threatens Mama releases her. We know that Jesus performed seven miracles of healing on the Sabbath day. Well, Father, today is the Sabbath, and we ask that He perform one more. We are lifting our eyes to the hills because that's where our help is coming from. We know that our help cometh from the Lord, and you are the only source right now. So here we are, Father, with our hands outstretched, touching the hem of your garment. We are leaning on you, oh Lord. We believe in our hearts that you can make an impossible situation possible. We ask that your will take place, Father. In the name of your son, Jesus Christ, amen."

CHAPTER 29
ADIEU, MON AMOUR

I 've never felt this kind of weight before. It feels like a ton of bricks are sitting right in the middle of my chest. I clutched my wife's warm hand. I'd never seen Faith this placid before but I know she's hurting. For the past week I've watched the light dim in her eyes. My lighthouse.

She's been quiet the whole service, barely even budged. Honestly, I don't blame her. This funeral has been a shit show. Where is the respect? Terrell and Chase took turns rambling on stage and calling on others to speak who had nothing to say when their mother was alive. All I've heard is Mama Frances was this and how she was like a mama to everyone. Man, fuck all that. Mama Frances looked for them in her time of need and saw no one. It's maddening that the woman who sacrificed her entire life for her family ended up this way. For years, Faith has told me that Mama Frances was the textbook definition of unconditional love. And after getting to know that beautiful lady over the years, I can agree. That's why loyalty is far more useful than love. Anyone can love. But love won't make a person do right. Loyalty, on the other hand, will make someone fight for you until the world blows up. With loyalty, someone will always stand by your side.

The attendant asks if anyone else would like to say something before they adjourn the service. Faith's feet move, and before I know it she's standing at the pulpit. She looks around the crowded room. I watch her watch her siblings hold each other and then register her mother's blank daze. Two rows ahead of me in the front row, Randy sits with bloodshot eyes. To his left is an exhausted Chase, who has finally stopped falling out. And next to him, Terrell. He sneers at Faith as though she couldn't possibly have anything better to say than what he has already. My body tingles with heat. I want nothing more than to go the hell off, releasing all her anger and frustrations for her. But what good would it do? No one would change. Or likely even comprehend the magnitude of what's happened. People will continue living their lives, never learning the lesson.

My wife locks eyes with me. I let them speak for me. "Breathe, baby. You got this."

"I just," Faith trails off, staring at the pearl white casket. Last night, she stood in the bathroom mirror brushing her teeth. She was frustrated. Her furrowed brows told me so. I saw a flash of heartbreak when she glanced at the mirror. I wanted to go to her, but she kept me at a distance. My wife has lost her way. Her true compass. At the pulpit, she seemed to register the same thought—just like that, my lighthouse went pitch black. Then tears spilled over and out like a volcano erupting. Before I knew it, my feet were standing beside hers. And my hands wiped at the wetness streaming down her face.

"Breathe, Faith. You got this. I got you."

ABOUT THE AUTHOR

B. J. Herron was born in Chicago and raised in the South Suburban area outside of the city. Growing up, she was fascinated with words and storytelling, and the meaning behind them. This interest led to some early exposure to reading since she was drawn to poetry and stories about people who looked like her. Later, B. J. received her MFA in Creative Writing from Full Sail University and worked for eleven years as a writer and editor for a myriad of publications, including the *Chicago Defender*. She now lives in Nashville, Tennessee. *Losing Love* is her first book.

CPSIA information can be obtained
at www.ICGtesting.com
Printed in the USA
LVHW012129300122
709678LV00004B/90